THE SECRET TO YOUR SURRENDER

ADELE CLEE

This is a work of fiction. All names, characters, places and incidents are products of the author's imagination. All characters are fictitious and any resemblance to real persons, living or dead, is purely coincidental.

No part of this book may be copied or reproduced in any manner without the author's permission.

Cover designed by **Jay Aheer**

Books by Adele Clee

To Save a Sinner

A Curse of the Heart

What Every Lord Wants

The Secret To Your Surrender

A Simple Case of Seduction

Anything for Love Series

What You Desire

What You Propose

What You Deserve

What You Promised

The Brotherhood Series

Lost to the Night

Slave to the Night

Abandoned to the Night

Lured to the Night

Lost Ladies of London

The Mysterious Miss Flint

The Deceptive Lady Darby

The Scandalous Lady Sandford

The Daring Miss Darcy

Avenging Lords

At Last the Rogue Returns

CHAPTER 1

$\mathcal{A}$nthony Dempsey, fifth Viscount Harwood, jumped up from the chair behind his mahogany desk and glared at his brother, Lucas. "Do you not think it appropriate to knock before you barge into a gentleman's study?"

"No. Not when I have had to drag myself away from Lord Daleforth's ball to come and search for you." Dressed immaculately in evening attire, Lucas folded his arms across his chest. "Are you not prepared to offer an explanation? Are you ill? Did you have a prior engagement you failed to mention?"

Anthony suppressed a sigh. "I had every intention of attending this evening." The lie fell easily from his lips though it left a bitter aftertaste that would taint his palate for hours. He gestured to the pile of papers scattered over the desk. "I simply lost all concept of time."

Lucas raised a dubious brow. "You are, or at least you were, the most reliable person I know." He shrugged. "Is it Miss Roxbury? Do you not wish to spend time in her company?"

The mere mention of her name roused an image of a

golden-haired goddess—a luscious, tempting beauty with the power to make a man lose his mind.

"I find her fascinating, utterly beguiling." That was not a lie. One glance and she had held him captive. "I've not the time nor the inclination to wed. It would be wrong to allow her to think otherwise."

"You no longer believe it is your duty to beget an heir?" Lucas asked incredulously.

Securing the family's heritage was a responsibility Anthony took seriously. He refused to be the foolish peer who let title and wealth cultivated through many generations slip through his fingers.

"You are my heir. Your son will one day be a viscount. Does the thought not please you?" He knew the answer to his question before noting Lucas' look of disdain.

Lucas gave an indolent wave. "Trust me. I do not regard it a blessing. How could I when you are shackled to your desk with no hope of reprieve?"

"I was born to shoulder responsibility." Duty, both the legal and moral obligation to one's family, was his birthright. "It is all I know."

"You are allowed some pleasure." Lucas stepped closer. "I want you to be happy. I do not want to walk in here and find a lonely, withered old man hunched over his desk."

Anthony chuckled though he found nothing amusing about his situation. "I have more than a few years before my eyesight fails me and my hair turns grey."

"Come with me," Lucas implored. "I shall wait while you change. Make your position clear to Miss Roxbury and enjoy her company as a friend."

A friend?

Friendship required a level of affection beyond his capabilities. In Miss Roxbury's company, he often found himself lost in wistful dreams of a dark, all-consuming passion, of a life filled with love and laughter.

"It is far too late to contemplate attending now," he said, his excuse feeble.

Lucas jerked his head back. "It is but ten o'clock. We'll arrive in plenty of time for supper."

"I will meet with you tomorrow."

There was a prolonged moment of silence.

"Helena begged me to come." Lucas' tone held a confidence in his ability to sway Anthony's decision. "I know how you hate to disappoint her. She will not sleep tonight unless she sees you and knows you are well."

Bloody hell!

His brother was a master of strategy and knew to wait to play his trump card.

"Your constant refusal to attend social functions is making her ill with worry," Lucas continued. "She fears you are suffering from an incurable malady and are attempting to avoid discovery."

"I am not ill," Anthony replied, knowing he was but seconds away from surrender. "I am sure you will find a way to placate her."

Lucas cast a look of reproach. "If that is what you wish me to tell her upon my return then so be it."

Age and position may have placed Anthony as head of the family, but Helena was the one who nurtured relationships. Since their mother's passing, Helena was the one who worked to strengthen bonds.

Guilt pricked his conscience.

In one respect, he supposed he *was* suffering from a malady. His secret was akin to a debilitating affliction that rendered him helpless. It lay buried inside the empty cavern of his chest, robbed him of all rational thought.

3

If he revealed the truth, Helena would berate him for his dishonesty. There was every chance she would not trust him again, her disappointment evident in her tone and manner whenever their paths crossed.

"You use your wife to force my hand. What next? No doubt little George is waiting in the hall with his nursemaid, a look of disappointment swimming in his eyes because his uncle has upset his mama."

An arrogant smile played at the corners of Lucas' mouth. "Damn. You know me so well."

He should have told Lucas to go to the devil, but he owed Helena a debt of gratitude that far outweighed the need to prove a point. Equally, it would not be wise to rouse her suspicions further. For a fleeting moment, he considered telling Lucas the truth but shook the idea away, along with the thought of spending a quiet night at home.

"Give me fifteen minutes," Anthony said as he strode to the door of his study. "And pour me a large glass of brandy while you wait."

He would need something to rid his mind of his pressing problems. Brandy would prove to be a far less complicated distraction than losing himself in Miss Roxbury's alluring gaze.

After paying his respects to Lord Daleforth and offering an apology for his late arrival, Anthony followed Lucas and went in search of Helena and her companions, the Roxburys.

They located Max Roxbury on the outskirts of the ball-room conversing with his wife, Prudence, while Helena sat in a chair only a foot away.

"Ah, the elusive Lord Harwood has appeared at last,"

Max said with a hint of amusement as he cast Anthony a side-long glance.

"It would not do to be too predictable," Anthony replied. "But in truth, I was waylaid with matters relating to estate business."

They did not need to raise their chins, twitch their brows or mutter between themselves for him to know they found his excuse far from convincing.

Lucas barged past them and crouched at Helena's side. "Are you well? You look pale." He stared into her eyes. "Perhaps you should have stayed at home this evening."

Anthony sighed. His brother was intent on proving his point.

"Nonsense." She gave an indolent wave and a weak chuckle. "I am tired that is all. But I did not want to miss the opportunity to spend time with my brother."

Guilt surfaced.

"Forgive me," Anthony said, coming to stand before her. He took Helena's gloved hand and brought it to his lips. "The last thing I want is to cause you distress."

Helena smiled. "Well, you are here now, though I am afraid Miss Roxbury grew tired of waiting and in your absence has taken to the dance floor."

Prudence cleared her throat. "Indeed. My sister is dancing with the Earl of Barton."

Barton? A frisson of fear coursed through Anthony's veins.

Despite all efforts to the contrary, it took but a few seconds for his gaze to drift to the couples gliding gracefully about the floor. It took but one glance for him to locate the lady who often plagued his dreams.

As though drawn by an undefinable force, he turned and took a few steps towards the open display of merriment.

Sarah Roxbury's golden hair shimmered in the candlelight as she swirled around the floor. Her cheeks were pink, flushed from exertion. Joy and happiness oozed from every fibre of her being, the fiery glow setting her apart from every other woman in the room. As did her smile, for it was pure, natural, free from artifice. Dazzling.

The muscles in his abdomen grew taut, tight. While lust clawed at his flesh like a savage beast, another emotion took precedence.

Jealousy.

The Earl of Barton held Sarah Roxbury's gloved hand in a talon-like grip. His beady stare dropped to the swell of smooth, creamy flesh visible above the neckline of her gown.

Anthony growled, albeit silently.

The need to claim the only woman he had ever wanted pushed to the fore. Murderous thoughts swamped him. His knuckles throbbed as he imagined landing a hard punch on the pompous lord's jaw. Though he considered the Earl of Barton an acquaintance, he was one of five gentlemen on Anthony's list of suspects.

Damn it all. He should not have come.

Lucas hovered at his side. "Standing there glaring will only add weight to the theory you have claimed Miss Roxbury for yourself."

Anthony snorted. "That sounds familiar. I recall saying the same thing to you once."

"Yes, and I married the lady in question."

"I do not intend to marry Miss Roxbury," Anthony whispered through gritted teeth. With the complicated nature of his problems, he could not marry anyone.

"You want her. It is blatantly obvious."

Were his feelings so transparent?

He was a man in control of his emotions. Exaggerated

displays of sentiment left one vulnerable, open to ridicule. In such cases, honesty proved challenging.

Anthony brushed his hand through his hair. "We cannot always have what we want."

"You are speaking to the wrong man if you're looking for sympathy. I see nothing other than pathetic excuses standing in your way."

Lucas would not feel the same way if he knew of the recent developments at Elton Park.

The music came to an end. The couples smiled and conversed as they took a moment to catch their breath. Anthony stared at Barton, studied every facial expression, every nuance, searching for clues.

What were his intentions towards Miss Roxbury?

Was he the one guilty of committing the heinous crimes?

Barton inclined his head to him as he edged past to escort Miss Roxbury back to the safety of her family.

"Ah, Harwood." The earl tapped him on the upper arm. "I have not seen you since that rather entertaining little gathering you had last year."

Was the gentleman trying to provoke him?

"I have been preoccupied of late," Anthony confessed. It took all his strength not to lock gazes with Miss Roxbury, yet he could feel her penetrating stare searching his face.

"I must thank you again, Lord Barton, for such a delightful turn about the floor." Miss Roxbury's flirtatious tone drifted through the air. Rather than soothe or excite it roused Anthony's ire.

"The pleasure was all mine," Barton replied in a sly, slippery way that revealed the lascivious nature of his thoughts. "Indeed, if you are not otherwise engaged, you may mark me down for another dance of your choosing."

Lucas coughed discreetly into his fist and raised a mocking brow.

Anthony swallowed down the hard lump beating wildly in his throat. Damn it all. The urge to punch the Earl of Barton took hold. Indeed, the ends of his fingers tingled and pulsed. His vision blurred. Harrowing images bombarded his mind: a golden-haired beauty protesting at the scoundrel's wandering hands, her screaming for help though no one could hear.

"I am certain I have space on my card," Miss Roxbury replied.

The first few strains of a waltz filtered through the hum of lively conversation. Fearing the earl would be bold enough to request his second dance immediately, Anthony stepped forward.

He held out his hand to her. "I believe if you examine your card you will find the next dance is mine, Miss Roxbury." The arrogant, rather rakish undercurrent to his tone was so unlike him.

To quash the thrum of desire, he told himself his motive for dancing was purely logical. The Earl of Barton could well be a murderous rogue intent on making even more mischief. Anthony valued Max Roxbury's friendship too much to place his wife's sister in danger.

Miss Roxbury's beguiling blue eyes focused on his hand.

There was a moment of silence. Anthony sensed her hesitation, wondered if she would call him to task for being so presumptuous.

When she inclined her head, all muscles in his body tensed to prepare for the internal battle soon to commence.

"I am surprised you remembered." Miss Roxbury's tone conveyed a hint of reproof. "You appear to be so forgetful of late."

She placed her dainty hand in his. Nothing prepared him

for the sudden rush of excitement. Nothing prepared him for the desperate pangs of longing pounding in his chest.

For the first time in his life, he wished he was his brother: a man with the strength and conviction to follow his heart. He wished he was a man without the crippling complications that would inevitably lead to a life of loneliness.

Suppressing a heavy sigh, he led Miss Roxbury out onto the floor, prayed he would survive the next five minutes. Come first light he would leave London and return to Elton Park. To remain would be akin to torture and he saw no end in sight to this form of self-flagellation.

Where Sarah Roxbury was concerned, it was time to accept Fate had chosen to direct them along different paths.

It was time to stop dreaming.

It was time to accept she could never be his.

CHAPTER 2

*T*he soothing melody of the waltz drifted through the ballroom though it did little to settle the nervous flutter in Sarah's stomach.

Since first meeting Viscount Harwood at Hagley Manor, she had found him to be a conundrum of mixed messages and conflicting manners. Had the gentleman been an identical twin who swapped places with his brother purely for amusement, it would have explained the unsettled nature of his character.

"So, this is to be our first dance, my lord." She spoke in the hope conversation would ease the mounting tension in the air.

While other couples glided about the floor, they stood still. The viscount stared at her, his expression unreadable. His hand hovered a mere inch from her waist, his hesitation apparent to all.

Why on earth had he requested to dance when clearly he found the thought repulsive?

"Dancing should be an enjoyable experience," she added,

offering a chuckle to disguise the odd pang of rejection, "not a distressing one."

He inclined his head. "Forgive me. It has been some time since I last took to the floor."

When his hot hand brushed her waist, she dismissed the wild rush of excitement coursing through her veins. The gentleman proved to be a disappointment on numerous occasions, and she refused to let hope blossom in her chest.

So why had she accepted his invitation to dance?

They had moved but a few feet when his hand became limp and flapped about on her lower back like a fish plucked from the water.

What was wrong with him?

"It is a waltz, my lord. If you refuse to hold me securely, there is every chance I shall stumble."

Sucking in a deep breath, he tightened his grip and pulled her close. A little too close. Like a torch to a flame, the surrounding air sparked to life. A soft gasp resonated in the back of her throat. The husky sound conveyed too much she feared.

The smile playing at the corners of his mouth revealed a switch was in progress. In an instant, the sullen brother retreated to the depths of his dark lair to skulk in the corner. His welcome departure made way for the confident, far more captivating twin.

"I am intrigued to know why you agreed to dance with me." His low, smooth voice was so different from the rigid, clipped tones she'd heard from him of late.

"Because you asked me to."

"But you knew I'd lied. My name was not on your card, yet you made no protest."

She pursed her lips. She had thought to humiliate him, to let him know how it felt to be treated coldly and with indifference. "I did not think it appropriate to embarrass you when in company. And truth be told, I had no desire to waltz with Lord Barton."

The downward curve of his mouth revealed an element of disappointment in her reply.

What did he expect her to say? That she so desperately wanted to know what it felt like to be held in his arms? That she enjoyed the shame of rejection and so chose to torture herself some more?

"Most ladies would be more than pleased to dance with an earl," he mocked. "Barton is a most eligible gentleman. His handsome countenance is said to enhance his appeal."

Handsome features were not on her list of necessary attributes though she could not deny, staring into Anthony Dempsey's mesmerising blue eyes often made her breathless.

"I am not like most ladies." Outwardly, she maintained her calm facade. Internally, her mind scrambled to understand the hidden meaning behind his comment. "Wealth and status are of no consequence to me."

Since Prudence had married Lord Roxbury, there was no longer any pressure to make a good match and save her poor siblings from a life of destitution.

Lord Harwood raised his brow with a look that suggested he doubted the truth of her conviction. "What, you would be happy to marry a butcher or baker?"

"I would be happy to marry a man I loved, regardless of all else."

His intense gaze drifted over her face, searching for something but she had no idea what. "And what is love to you, Miss Roxbury?"

His slow, purposeful drawl caused her heart to flutter in her chest. Heavens. How was she to respond to such a probing question?

"Do you … do you speak of love for one's family or a different sort of love?"

He stared at her mouth. "I speak of love between a man and a woman. The kind mused over by poets, depicted in plays."

"How can I answer when I have never experienced the emotion to that degree?" She was intrigued to know if he had ever been in love. "Perhaps you should offer your wisdom on the subject." She had observed his stony silence many times. It made a refreshing change for him to converse with such enthusiasm.

A mischievous smile touched his lips. It lit up his face, made him appear a little wicked, dare she admit far more intriguing. "Love is a feeling foreign to me, too. But I expect that to love a woman means to care about her welfare over and above your own."

She could not help but giggle. His explanation proved to be sensible, yet lacked any real depth of emotion. "What a romantic you are, my lord. No wonder it has been an age since you took to the floor."

"What, you do not agree?"

"Of course I agree. But you could have spoken about a grand passion, infused your words with a deep sense of long-ing. You could have said you expect love to be a pleasurable agony that plagues you mind and body, that you would need the object of your affection like you need air to breathe."

Good Lord. In her eagerness to prove her point she had said far too much.

"While my explanation may have lacked clarity, Miss Roxbury, you have conveyed your thoughts clearly."

The strange tugging sensation in her stomach returned. What was this mysterious power that held her captive in his presence? An invisible barrier of unspoken words and unnamed emotions existed between them. The thought of stepping into uncharted territory released a warm wave of energy capable of robbing her of all rational thought.

She gave a weak smile, grateful to hear the last few notes of the waltz playing out. An end to this delicious form of torment was in sight. But while other couples parted and paid joyous thanks to their companions, Anthony Dempsey did not relinquish his grip.

"Our dance has come to an end, my lord." A rising blush forced her to speak. The gentleman's puzzling behaviour hurt her head.

He released her, blinked and sighed. "Thank you, Miss Roxbury, for a rather enlightening experience."

Drifting from the floor in a cloud of confusion, it wasn't until she reached the Dempseys that she realised she was holding her breath.

"We were waiting for you to return," Helena said as she stood and took her husband's arm. "Max and Prudence decided to take a turn about the garden."

"I thought we could join them." Lucas Dempsey addressed his brother. "Helena is in need of some air, and I agreed we would not leave Miss Roxbury unattended. As you are not engaged to dance with anyone else, I assume you won't mind joining us."

The muscle in Anthony Dempsey's cheek twitched. For a moment, Sarah thought he might refuse. Well, she'd be damned before he would make a fool of her again. Indeed, she was about to offer a protest when Helena stepped closer.

"I know it is not a topic of conversation for the ballroom," she whispered, "or any other room for that matter. But my delicate condition deems I must take a short stroll."

The mix of pride and pain etched on Lucas Dempsey's

face supported Helena's revelation. "My wife has only just seen fit to inform me of the news."

Sarah glanced at Lord Harwood whose pale face and rigid countenance was no doubt a common sight on any surgeon's table. Despite his obvious reluctance to walk outdoors, he smiled, offered his felicitations to the couple and conveyed his pleasure at the prospect of becoming an uncle for the second time.

"Please say you will join us?" Helena said.

How could they refuse?

Lord Harwood inhaled deeply before offering his arm. "Would you care to accompany me on a stroll around the gardens, Miss Roxbury?"

There was a moment of silence while they anticipated her answer. Sarah stared into Lord Harwood's eyes, saw the glassy, glazed look he used to shield emotion.

For her sanity, she should decline. "I am sure a stroll will be a pleasant distraction."

Lord Harwood straightened. "Shall we?"

Dismissing all doubts her fingers settled on his muscular arm. "C-certainly."

The Dempseys gestured for them to lead the way. Lord Harwood steered her out through the terrace doors and onto a meandering gravel path.

The cool, crisp night air brought instant relief. A light breeze drifted over her and blew at the wispy curls framing her face. It calmed her mind, eased her anxiety.

"Are you cold?"

She glanced across the manicured lawn, at the attendant topiary, at anything other than the man at her side. "No. I find the slight chill rather refreshing."

"I agree. I often walk around the grounds of Elton Park after sunset," he said, his tone subdued. "The night is a time for reflection. It is a time when the world is at peace. When one's soul may experience a similar sense of harmony."

An image of a solitary man wandering aimlessly through the garden appeared in her mind, the figure nothing but a sad shadow against the vast expanse.

"It is strange the effect nature can have on one's person," she said, desperate to lighten the mood. "I have often thought the wind is nought but a collection of people's whispered words, of muttered dreams and aspirations carried forth in the hope someone will hear them."

There was a moment of silence.

"It is an interesting concept," he said. "In one respect, giving one's dreams wings to fly creates an element of hope that they exist beyond the restrictions we place upon them, that they are not hampered by our fears and doubts."

After such an insightful response, Sarah could not help but sneak a peek at his profile. On the surface he appeared relaxed, comfortable, in control. Yet beneath the mask, a dark unknown emotion lingered. Was it grief, fear, despair? She could not tell.

"And what does a gentleman possessed of title and good fortune dream about?"

"I am a simple man, Miss Roxbury. I dream of simple things. Yet by definition, dreams are thought to be unobtainable." The heat from his penetrating stare warmed her cheeks. To meet his gaze would be a mistake. "But what of you? What does a lady possessed of elegance and beauty dream about?"

While most ladies would revel in such a compliment, it was important he understood she was more than the sum of her facial features.

"I dream of studying the stars, of understanding the true meaning of our existence." She looked up to the heavens. "I want to read philosophy, ponder over the theories, yet have the courage to draw my own conclusions."

Excitement fluttered in her breast. Saying the words aloud made it feel as though her thoughts had sprouted wings and taken flight. She stopped walking. Hidden by the shadows of the tall topiary hedge she turned to face him, determined to make her point.

"I want to help those less fortunate, to teach the children from poor families to read and write, find ways to encourage them to hope and dream, too." She could not help but chuckle. "I want a great many things, my lord, though I have never told another soul."

She made the mistake of staring into those brilliant blue eyes. His gaze was intense, hungry, ready to devour her and savour every morsel.

"Most ladies would dream of pretty bonnets and priceless bracelets. I find your revelation refreshing." His rich tone caused the hairs at her nape to tingle. "But in your eagerness to reveal your innermost thoughts you did not mention love."

"We … we all want to love and be loved in return." She swallowed to dislodge the lump in her throat. "Love is surely the greatest gift of all."

"Indeed, I am inclined to agree."

Something happened in that moment. A connection formed. There was an element of clarity where their dreams and desires aligned. The sound of their laboured breathing filled the air. The wind whistled past them, whispering words of hope, of freedom—a promise that these confounding emotions could develop into something wonderful.

When his gaze fell to her mouth, she moistened her lips.

He was going to kiss her.

The anticipation sent a rush of raw emotion to excite every nerve and fibre of her being. She glanced to her right, noted that the Dempseys had stopped walking and were engaged in examining the foliage. When Lord Harwood captured her hands, she feared her knees would buckle.

He lowered his head, his face a mere inch from hers. The scents of shaving soap and clean linen were obliterated by an intoxicating essence she could not define. Just when she expected to feel the light brushing of his lips, he turned his head away, stared at the ground while still holding on to her hands.

A sharp stab of disappointment flared in her chest. Frustration gave way to anger, only to be replaced by shame and an overwhelming feeling of inadequacy.

Sarah tugged her hands from his grasp. Tears formed in her eyes. She wanted to let them fall, to let him know his unpredictable behaviour hurt her. But she refused to be seen as a weak woman, one desperate for an opportunity to be kissed.

"It is not wise to be out here for so long." Her voice sounded fractured, croaky. Damn him. She gestured to Helena and Lucas Dempsey who were now engaged in examining the facade of Lord Daleforth's townhouse. "And my chaperones are somewhat lacking when it comes to supervision."

"Miss Roxbury—"

"Let us return to the ballroom." To hear him spout words of logic and reason was more than she could bear. "The temperature has dropped considerably." She wrapped her arms around her chest to ward off the frosty chill in the air though the action did little to ease the ache in her heart.

Lord Harwood inclined his head but said nothing.

They walked back along the path in strained silence though her inner voice mocked her incessantly for her folly. When they caught up with the Dempseys, she suppressed a sigh of relief.

Helena's inquisitive gaze passed back and forth between them. "Please tell me you are not eager to return to the stuffy confines of the ballroom? We have been outdoors for mere minutes."

"It is a little too cold tonight," Sarah replied. With her fluctuating body temperature, she was liable to catch a fever. "And I must visit the retiring room." She needed to catch her breath, to settle her erratic thoughts, to stare into the looking glass and find the courage to admit she deserved more than Anthony Dempsey could ever give.

CHAPTER 3

*G*od, he was a damn fool.

Anthony had spent the best part of two weeks avoiding any close contact with Sarah Roxbury. When alone, he could rationalise his feelings. Control was a skill he had honed. Yet something about the lady spoke to him as no other woman had done before. For the first time in his life, temptation proved too great. Indeed, it had taken every ounce of strength he possessed not to devour her mouth as he'd dreamed of doing too many times to count.

As he stood in the ballroom waiting for Miss Roxbury and Helena to return from the retiring room, he glanced at his pocket watch. Soon they would serve supper. He would offer an excuse and make a hasty retreat.

"Miss Roxbury appears eager to be free of your company." Lucas' tone brimmed with reproof. "Can you not try to be a little more endearing?"

Endearing?

He had come close to ravishing the lady in the garden.

"I made my position clear when you charged into my home and dragged me from my study." Guilt surfaced,

20

forcing him to clench his teeth to convey his point. "God damn, why can you not leave things alone? Forcing us to spend time together will only ruin Miss Roxbury's chances of making a match."

The thought of her marrying any other man was akin to a blunt blade stabbing at his heart.

Lucas frowned. "What the hell has happened to you?"

"I do not know what you mean."

"You're different. Permanently preoccupied. And do not dare say it is due to estate business. If your issue with Miss Roxbury stems from your over-cautious nature, then—"

"To be cautious is to be wise." Anthony straightened. "Prudence is a trait I admire."

"No. You're hiding something." Lucas pursed his lips. "Have you financial worries? Because if you do, you know I will help."

"I am more than capable of managing the estate."

Lucas folded his arms across his chest and studied him. "Ride with me in the park tomorrow—"

"Riding in the park," Helena interrupted as she appeared at their side. "How wonderful. We shall all go. Mrs Reed can arrange a picnic …"

Helena continued talking, but Anthony stopped listening. His gaze drifted past Helena's shoulder. But the object of his desire had vanished.

"Where is Miss Roxbury?" He could not hide the slight hint of panic in his voice as he scanned the colourful sea of heads.

Helena glanced back over her shoulder. "Well, she was walking behind me." She stood on the tips of her toes and searched the crowd. "Wait. Oh, there she is. It is such a crush in here tonight. And I fear Miss Roxbury is often far too polite for her own good."

Anthony sighed, albeit silently. Relief coursed through him. He did not trust Barton. A woman as alluring as Miss Roxbury would prove to be an amusing game for the cads.

"Good heavens." Miss Roxbury struggled to catch her breath as she came to join them. "I thought they would never let me through." Her hand came to rest on her heaving bosom. The rapid rise and fall of creamy flesh proved to be too much of a distraction.

Bloody hell!

Anthony swallowed deeply. Surely it was time for the supper gong.

"People can be so rude," Helena said, patting Miss Roxbury affectionately on the arm. "I've often thought of arming myself with a hat pin and prodding them in the rear."

Miss Roxbury chuckled. "*Rude* is far too polite a term. I had to shove a gentleman in the back and still he seemed oblivious to my predicament. But then the strangest thing occurred." The lady raised her hand in such a dramatic fashion one expected her to perform a magician's trick. Slowly, she unfurled her clenched fist to reveal a single, smooth black feather.

Like sustaining a hard punch to the gut, all the air was sucked from Anthony's lungs. He resisted the urge to clutch his throat and gasp for breath. He stared at the ominous object lying in the delicate palm of her hand, unable to form a coherent thought let alone a word.

"It's a feather," Helena said, somewhat bemused. "How on earth did you come by it?"

"That is what's so strange. Someone touched my hand, pressed the feather into my palm and forced my fingers to make a fist." Miss Roxbury shook her head. The golden curls framing her face bobbed up and down. Amusement flashed in her bright blue eyes, yet terror crept through

Anthony's veins ready to claw at his heart. "It was most bizarre."

"Did this person say anything?" Helena said, her tone revealing how she thrived on intrigue. "Did they offer an explanation?"

"No. And when I turned to see if I could locate the culprit, there was no one there."

Lucas snorted. "No doubt it fell out of a lady's elaborate coiffure and this person assumed it was yours. Perhaps it was their intention to speak, but found themselves jostled along with the crowd."

Helena raised a brow. "Have you ever seen a lady wearing an ugly black feather in her hair? Besides, it is far too small to make an impact."

"It could be part of an ensemble of numerous shades. It could have belonged to a hair comb." Lucas smiled and inclined his head. "But as you rightly said, I am not an expert in ladies' fripperies." He glanced at the tiny row of pearls edging the low neckline of Helena's gown. "Perhaps you might see fit to educate me in the use of trinkets as an adornment."

A smile played at the corners of Helena's mouth.

"I imagine it was stuck to someone's shoe, and they thought it an amusing distraction to thrust it into my hand," Miss Roxbury added.

They were all wrong.

The feather was a warning—a threat.

He was here—tonight—in the ballroom.

The Earl of Barton had made his attendance known. But then any one of the other four gentlemen could be hiding in the shadows.

Anthony glanced covertly around the room. Being out in Society created a feeling of vulnerability that did not sit well with him. The scoundrel was watching him. And there was not a damn thing he could do about it.

"Yes, it looks like a bird's breast feather." Helena's comment disturbed his reverie.

"It is the breast feather of a blackbird," Anthony informed. "And I am inclined to agree with Miss Roxbury," he lied. "Someone brought it in from the garden."

After weeks spent researching the symbolic meaning, he knew why the blackguard taunted him with that particular feather. If one was to believe in myth and lore, blackbirds were the keepers of secrets. They brought a warning that one must protect what is theirs.

The feather also represented desire.

It was said the Devil once took on the form of a black-bird to torment St. Benedict. Soon after, the man developed an intense sexual desire for a girl. It was said he stripped naked and jumped into a thorn bush, that pain and suffering was the only way to rid him of all temptation.

The pain of loss and the crippling sense of loneliness was the price Anthony had to pay to protect everything dear to him.

"You see," Lucas said. "Here we are rambling on about combs and the like and my brother puts us all to shame with his simple yet logical explanation."

"As you know," Anthony began, "I have never been one for fanciful musings." That was another lie. Since meeting Sarah Roxbury, he had developed an addiction for daydreaming.

"Well," Helena began, her face alight with excitement, "I am more inclined to believe it is a sign."

Anthony held his breath.

"It is a sign we need to spend more time outdoors,"

Helena continued, "and so we have no option but to take a picnic to the park tomorrow."

The sound of the supper gong rang through the room. The clanging vibration brought a collective gasp from the throng. For Anthony, it brought an immense sense of relief.

The carriage rumbled to a halt at the side of the road. Through the window, Anthony watched Miss Roxbury alight from her conveyance and the sunny day suddenly appeared much brighter. She rushed over to greet Helena who was waiting at the gates leading into the park.

Anthony rubbed his chin and sighed. A deep sense of regret enveloped him. It was not in his nature to be a disappointment. But then he could not risk them discovering he was a man being held to ransom for one stupid mistake.

Miss Roxbury smiled and made numerous animated gestures. They laughed. Prudence Roxbury came to join them with two footmen in tow carrying overladen baskets.

Lucas and Max Roxbury appeared, sitting astride their horses. Anthony felt a pang of guilt as he witnessed his brother pull out his pocket watch and check the time. Lucas scanned his surroundings before staring at the small round face with some confusion.

He could not risk them recognising his carriage. Lucas had the verbal ability to convince a nun to sin, and Anthony did not wish to cause any more distress.

With the tip of his walking cane, he hit the roof of his conveyance twice. Carter responded instantly and within seconds the vehicle lurched forward, and they were soon rattling along on their way out of the city.

Road and weather permitting, they would cover the fifty-mile journey to Witham in a little less than five hours. It would give him time to think, time to formulate a plan. The incident with the feather had forced him to confront the truth.

The bastard knew his every move, would hound him till he gasped his last breath. What then? Would he threaten Lucas in the same cowardly fashion? Would his brother and nephew forever live in fear, be tainted by scandal?

God damn it. Anthony had to do something. He was a viscount. A peer of the realm. A man of honour.

But where to start?

The beginning was the obvious answer.

The crime scene was just as Anthony had left it on that fateful day, five months earlier. To his knowledge, no one had entered the stone cottage. Many a night he had opened the gate and crept along the overgrown path, hovered at the small wooden door to settle his stomach. Yet his hand lacked the strength to turn the handle. He did not need to look upon the grisly sight to remind him of all that had occurred. The gruesome images plagued his thoughts, were forever there in the background, haunting him.

Releasing a weary sigh, he dragged his hand down his face.

If he was to learn anything, he must detach himself emotionally. Logical thinking required a clear mind. A mind encumbered by the cobwebs of the past proved useless when it came to detailed analysis. While he was lost in thoughtful contemplation, the journey home passed quickly.

"Welcome home, my lord." Chadwick inclined his head, ensuring his spectacles remained firmly on his nose.

"Thank you, Chadwick." Anthony handed the butler his hat and gloves. A quick glance at the metal rims sitting crookedly on his servant's face confirmed he was still struggling to get used to the eyeglasses. "Will you inform Mrs Adams I'd like to speak to her in the study?"

"Certainly, my lord. Will you be dining at eight?"

Anthony glanced at the long-case clock in the hall. It was almost seven. "Eight would be perfect. How are you finding your new spectacles?"

"They are a blessing, my lord, as long as I do not move my head. Naturally, that proves to be a slight problem on occasion."

"Well, it is better than walking into the newel post," Anthony replied, suppressing a chuckle.

"That it is, my lord." Chadwick bowed. "I believe Mrs Adams is with Mrs Russell in the … the small bedchamber. I shall send her down at once."

Growing accustomed to spectacles was not the only new addition his butler struggled to accept. Anthony wondered if the old man had made any progress in dealing with their houseguest.

"On second thoughts, Chadwick, I shall go in search of Mrs Adams myself. It is only fitting I inform Mrs Russell of my return."

Chadwick maintained his blank expression. "Then I shall inform Cook of the evening's schedule, my lord."

With a slow, solemn gait, Chadwick retreated. Anthony climbed the stairs to the first floor, strode purposefully along the hallway only to meet his housekeeper outside the bedchamber door.

"My lord." Mrs Adams curtsied. "I trust you had a pleasant journey."

"Pleasant, yet somewhat tiring." He had spent two hours thinking of a plan to solve his predicament, three hours dreaming of a golden-haired temptress with a mouth sweet enough to banish all his troubles. He glanced over his housekeeper's shoulder at the bedchamber door. "I assume everything is in order, and Mrs Russell is proving satisfactory."

"All is well, my lord," she said, straightening her white cap. "Mrs Russell likes routine, and we have all learnt to make adjustments. You'll not be troubled. You'll not even know they're here."

"May I go in?"

"Of course, my lord." Mrs Adams stepped to the side. "The wet nurse has returned to the village and will be back in the morning. Mrs Russell is settling the child."

"You made it clear the child is my ward?"

"I did, my lord, the son of a relative on your mother's side who recently met with a tragic accident."

The child's mother had indeed met with more than her fair share of tragedy. "Thank you, Mrs Adams."

Anthony opened the door and crept inside.

Mrs Russell acknowledged him with a curtsy, gestured to the crib and left the room.

He stood over the crib for a while, clutched the smooth wooden edge and watched the child's eyes flutter open as he struggled to sleep. The rhythmical sound of his peaceful breathing brought an element of calm to Anthony's erratic thoughts.

Taking a peek back over his shoulder, Anthony leant down and gathered the babe up into his arms. The boy cooed, blinked and smiled in response. The tip of his tongue brushed his upper lip: a sign he expected feeding.

"I'm afraid I cannot help on that score."

The child wrapped his tiny hand around Anthony's finger and held on tight. For such a small thing, his grip was remarkably strong.

"I know what it is like to crave love," he said, purely to speak to someone who could not answer back or offer words of wisdom. "I know what it feels like to be without that one special person who makes life worth living."

As always, a deep feeling of sorrow filled his chest, though bitterness and anger soon pushed to the surface.

"Your mama and papa have a lot to answer for," he whispered as he rocked the boy gently back and forth, though Emily Compton would never be able to make amends for what she had done.

Emily Compton was dead.

CHAPTER 4

"I do not think it is a good idea." Sarah sat perched on the edge of the chair in the Dempseys' drawing room, holding her hands rigid in her lap for it was the only way to control her volatile emotions. "Lord Harwood obviously wishes to be left alone in peace."

To arrive at Elton Park unannounced spoke of desperation. While she found the lord charming on occasion, handsome and intriguing most of the time, recognised the spark of attraction that flared between them, she refused to suffer the humiliation.

"My brother does not know what he wants." Lucas Dempsey folded his arms across his chest and sighed. "There is something on his mind. It must be important for him to behave so selfishly."

For the third time in less than a week, Viscount Harwood had failed to keep an appointment. The time for being polite and biting one's tongue had passed.

"Forgive me for saying so, but what right have we to interfere? Lord Harwood is a gentleman of great responsibility, a deep thinker. From his actions it is apparent he prefers his own company, and I must respect his wishes."

She refused to ride up to the door of Elton Park only to witness disdain or, even worse, indifference.

Mr Dempsey sat forward. "I believe it is his preoccupation with respectability that prevents him from revealing the truth. He is troubled. I am convinced something ails him."

"Then as his brother, you must go to him. You must try your utmost to help. You must persuade him to confide in you." It was what she would do for her siblings. She sat up straight. "I cannot go. Indeed, I intend to leave for Hagley Manor first thing in the morning."

Prudence gasped. "Hagley Manor? But you were so keen to come to town."

Sarah's eagerness had stemmed from the hope of meeting Lord Harwood again. During her stay in London, only one man had captured her interest. Only one man had the ability to touch her soul with a single glance.

"I want to go home, for a month maybe two." It would take considerably longer for her to forget the way Lord Harwood made her feel. "Perhaps I could attend a provincial ball, return to London next Season."

Or perhaps not at all.

Prudence glanced at Helena. A look passed between them. They may as well have jumped up from their chairs and shouted, "Good Lord! She's in love with him!"

Well, she was not in love with Anthony Dempsey. Most of the time she did not even like him. Besides, one could not love a man who proved to be a constant disappointment.

Prudence turned to Max who appeared bored with the conversation. "Perhaps we should go home. No doubt Grandpapa and the girls would welcome our return. After all, we came here to introduce Sarah into Society and if she is unhappy—"

"I am not unhappy," Sarah countered, "and I am extremely grateful to you all." But she was tired, weary. Her bruised heart needed time to heal. And for some unknown reason, other men were as appealing as rotten fruit in a broken basket.

Max brushed his hand through his hair and sighed. "Well, you know my feelings on the matter. There is not a gentleman in London who does not appreciate Sarah's exceptional qualities." He smiled at her affectionately. "You will know when the time is right for you to make a match. When you do, there will be no end of gentlemen lining up for the privilege."

Lining up? Max made her sound like a pig in a pen at Smithfield Market. It was the best place in the world for a man to purchase meat.

"You will all stay for dinner?" Helena said, changing the subject.

Max cleared his throat. "As it is to be our last night in town, I'm sure I can speak for everyone when I say there is no place we would rather be."

Sarah had just climbed into bed when there was a tap at her bedchamber door.

Prudence peeked inside. "Oh, good. I feared you might be asleep." Her sister slipped into the room, closed the door and came to sit on the edge of the bed. "I wanted to talk to you before we leave for Hagley Manor in the morning."

Sarah suppressed a sigh. "If it is about Lord Harwood then I would rather you didn't."

Prudence grasped her hand. "I know you care for the

viscount. I have seen the way your eyes sparkle when you look at him, noticed the way your lips tremble when you speak. If it is not true, then tell me I have made a mistake, and I shall never mention him again."

Just thinking about Anthony Dempsey caused a strange flutter in her chest. Though try as she might, she could not lie to her sister. "No. You have not made a mistake. But it is plain to see the gentleman is not capable of intimacy."

Well, that was not entirely accurate. In the garden, she had sensed a wave of emotion swell and surge deep within him. Indeed, she would have been swept away had he not had a sudden change of heart and decided not to kiss her.

"I think you're wrong." Prudence shook her head. "I have seen the way he looks at you, too. I agree with Mr Dempsey. Something is troubling the viscount, and I fear that is the reason for his austere facade."

Sarah doubted there was a lady alive in the world who would tolerate his odd moods. "For my sanity and the need for self-preservation, I cannot continue to wait in the hope that he will one day wake from his strange stupor and decide he cares."

Prudence frowned. "I do agree. And I know I jest about the need for you to make an advantageous match, but I want you to be happy. I want you to marry for love."

"I want those things, too, which is why I cannot continue to foster any hope where Lord Harwood is concerned." Tears threatened to form. "I must forget about him, Prue."

Prudence covered her mouth with her hands and sat silently for a moment. "Why don't you go with the Dempseys to Elton Park?" she suddenly blurted. "They only plan to stay for a few days. Helena will be your chaperone and no one need know of your visit. Give Mr Dempsey an opportunity to help his brother. And if the situation remains the same, then you will return to Hagley Manor as planned."

Prudence did not know what she was asking. To see Lord Harwood at home, relaxed and comfortable, would only feed the dull ache of disappointment.

"I would offer to accompany you," Prudence continued, "but with a house full of guests, I fear Mr Dempsey will not get the opportunity to uncover the root cause of the problem."

Sarah doubted there was a problem. Perhaps the lord simply had no inclination to marry. No doubt he was tired of people forcing his hand and had escaped to the country at the first opportunity.

"Don't ask it of me, Prue. Not when you would have stamped on Lord Harwood's toe and thrown a vase of water over his head for his conflicting manners and opinions."

Prudence chuckled. "Well, I would not have gone that far, but you're right. At the very least, I would have put a pine cone on his chair at dinner."

Sarah put her fingers to her lips to stifle a yawn. "I should get some sleep. We have an early start in the morning, and Kitty still hasn't finished packing my trunk."

"Very well. Will you promise to consider what I've said?"

Sarah gave a weak smile. "I will consider all you have said." When lying alone at night, she rarely thought of anything else.

Prudence stood. She hovered near the bed. The prominent lines between her brows and her puffed cheeks indicated there was more she wanted to say. With a weary sigh, her sister turned and took a few steps towards the door before swinging back round.

"But what if this is your only chance of finding true love, and you let it slip through your fingers? What if no other man will ever compare to Lord Harwood? To spend a lifetime living with regret would be unbearable. Do you not owe it to yourself to try one last time?"

A sudden surge of emotion forced Sarah to jump out of bed. She took hold of her sister's hands. "He doesn't want me, Prue." A sharp stab in her chest forced her to chuckle. "You will have to accept I may have to marry for money."

Prudence pulled her into an embrace. "You're wrong. I think he wants you more than you could possibly know. I think he wants you so much it pains him to spend time in your company."

Hope blossomed in Sarah's chest.

An image of them together formed in her mind. In the moment of fancy, she could feel Anthony Dempsey's arms wrapped around her. She conjured the intoxicating scent that clung to his skin and enveloped her whenever he was close. She imagined the taste of his lips. She heard his declaration of love.

The dream sprouted tiny wings and took flight. Sarah glanced at the window despite the closed drapes. Somewhere out there, her dream was drifting through the night sky, being carried on a gentle breeze, waiting for Fate to pluck it out of obscurity.

Somewhere hope still existed.

CHAPTER 5

"*L*et me take my son for a moment." Lucas Dempsey shuffled to the edge of his seat as the carriage rumbled along the narrow country lane. The boy found the springy ride amusing and insisted on bouncing up and down on his nursemaid's lap. Mr Dempsey held out his arms to the servant who seemed more than grateful to hand over the lively toddler.

"He appears to be enjoying the journey," Sarah said, suppressing a chuckle at the maid's faint sigh of relief.

Mr Dempsey's eyes sparkled with amusement. "I'm afraid he has his mother's stubbornness and his father's utter lack of propriety. Heaven help us should we ever have a daughter."

Delighted to be in his father's arms, the boy spent the next few minutes tugging on the ends of the gentleman's impeccable cravat.

Despite the jovial shrieks and the erratic rocking, Helena slept.

"Either the motion has unsettled your stomach or the thought of seeing my brother leaves you terrified," Mr

Dempsey said as he stared at Sarah from the opposite side of the carriage. "He will welcome us. You have no need to worry on that score."

Were her doubts and fears so apparent?

"I am the last person he will expect to see." Indeed, like a disappointed parent, the voice of reason insisted on berating her for the foolish decision to travel to Elton Park. Prudence had conveyed nothing but delight at her sudden change of heart, insisting everything would work out perfectly.

If only Sarah had her sister's confidence.

"I want you to know I appreciate the effort it has taken for you to accompany us," Mr Dempsey said as though he had read her thoughts. "My brother has always been the calm, rational one. Indeed, I have always looked to him for support and advice." He glanced briefly at the nursemaid. "I fear he is not himself of late, and I ask you to bear that in mind during our stay."

Sarah had witnessed many facets to the viscount's character. Even when he appeared distant and disinterested, something inside drew her to him. The urge to soothe away his woes kept her awake most nights.

Sarah offered a reassuring smile. "Well, sir, I have a strong constitution. Regardless of your brother's efforts to ignore me, I hope to be of some help."

"Indeed." A mischievous smile played at the corners of Mr Dempsey's mouth. "I am certain you will be the perfect distraction." He cast a sidelong glance at Helena whose head was now resting on his shoulder. "I never underestimate the power of a lady determined to show a gentleman what is important."

He looked at his wife as though he would spill blood for her, die to keep her safe. His tone, coupled with the words he did not need to say, gave the impression she was the rarest of gifts, precious, irreplaceable.

Sarah suppressed a sigh.

Would Anthony Dempsey ever look at her in the same way?

The deep sense of longing caused her heart to beat wildly in her breast. This was to be her last chance of finding happiness. Coming to Elton Park could be the worst mistake of her life. It was imperative she knew when to accept defeat, and when to walk away.

"And your offer still stands, sir," she clarified, eager to hear Mr Dempsey's assurance.

The gentleman inclined his head. "At any point during your stay you may leave. My coachman, Jackson, will deliver you safely back to Hagley Manor."

While Sarah spent the last few minutes of their journey in silence, Mr Dempsey settled his son on his lap and pointed at the window, repeating the names of various passing objects.

As the carriage charged through the Grecian-inspired stone gateway, all the air dissipated from her lungs. In a few minutes she would face the man whose voice soothed her soul, whose heated gaze robbed her of all logical thought. What would she say to him? Would the words tumble from her mouth in a torrent of incoherent nonsense?

The vast mansion came into view. The Doric columns of the front portico stretched higher than the first-floor windows. It created a grand, domineering presence, rigid and forthright.

The nature of its commanding position on the flat, green landscape instilled a strong sense of ownership, yet she could not help but see it as something cold, isolated, alone.

"Goodness. We're here." Helena stretched her arms as she peered out of the carriage window. "Have I slept for that long?"

Mr Dempsey cast a wicked grin. "You have been muttering and mumbling for hours." He brushed a loose tendril of hair from Helena's face. The intimacy of the moment made Sarah reach for the door handle.

A footman appeared, lowered the steps and held on to the tips of her gloved fingers until her feet touched the gravel and she was confident her legs would support her weight.

"Ah, Chadwick." Mr Dempsey stepped out of the carriage as the butler came down the three stone steps to meet him. "New spectacles?"

"I'm afraid they are a necessity, sir." The butler bowed, albeit a little awkwardly. His tight lips were drawn thin as he greeted them all. "I was forever tripping over the steps."

Mr Dempsey chuckled. "I assume my brother is at home."

"His lordship is in the study, sir, though he asked—"

"Excellent. No need to show us the way, Chadwick. But would you mind escorting Miss Davis to find Mrs Adams? George has spent the best part of five hours cooped up in the carriage and needs somewhere quiet to take a nap."

Mr Dempsey did not give the old man an opportunity to comment. He led them through the entrance hall, past a sculpture she recognised as Mercury, God of Travellers, past a row of shiny marble pillars and a grand staircase.

Everything, from the quality of the furnishings to the condition of the decor, was of the highest standard. Despite its austere facade, the house was well kept, felt cherished, loved.

They stopped outside a large oak door.

"One must have courage when stepping into the lair of a dragon," Helena whispered, placing a comforting hand on Sarah's arm.

Mr Dempsey raised a brow and grinned. "This particular

dragon has forgotten how to breathe fire, and so we must remind him of all he is missing."

Helena grinned too. "Remember, Miss Roxbury, to show fear will make him feel superior. Dragons like to be put in their place as it makes for a far more interesting encounter. And never forget, honesty is always the best policy."

Mr Dempsey nodded. "There is nothing as alluring as the truth, Miss Roxbury."

Sarah stared at them. They really were the most amusing couple.

Mr Dempsey knocked the door and without waiting for a response entered the room.

"What is it, Chadwick?" the viscount snapped. "I recall asking not to be disturbed under any circumstances."

Lord Harwood did not look up from the pile of papers strewn over his desk. The untidy spectacle appeared so out of place in a room that was pristine and orderly. He sat in his shirtsleeves, the white linen rolled up to the elbows to reveal the dark hair covering his forearms. His dark locks were a little wild and unruly. Studying his profile, Sarah noted the faint shadow gracing his cheeks where he had failed to shave.

In his private lair, Anthony Dempsey was a perfect picture of rugged masculinity.

Sarah swallowed down the sudden rush of excitement that sought to rob her of breath.

"I hoped you would make an exception for family," Mr Dempsey said.

The lord's gaze shot up from his papers. "Lucas. What are you doing here?" Deep trenches formed on his brow. His mouth opened and closed a few times, but he failed to form another word.

"Well, I grew tired of waiting at the park and thought it best to come and find you."

The viscount stood up, ran his fingers through his hair and patted his chest. "I am not dressed to receive visitors. You should have sent word you were coming."

"What, so you could bar the doors and retreat to the dungeon?"

Lord Harwood shuffled the papers into a rough pile before coming around the desk to greet them.

"Helena, I trust you had a pleasant journey." He bowed to his sister-in-law, but she stepped closer and rubbed his upper arms affectionately, touched the bristles gracing his chin.

"It was so pleasant, I slept most of the way," Helena said with a chuckle. "You look as though you slept on your desk."

"I had plans to oversee." He waved at the mess behind him. "It took a little longer than I anticipated."

Sarah sucked in a breath when Lord Harwood moved to stand in front of her. The corners of his mouth twitched into the beginnings of a smile though she sensed his unease.

He inclined his head. "Forgive my rather crude appearance, Miss Roxbury. Had I known you were coming I would have made myself more presentable."

Try as she might, she could not calm her racing heart. She wanted to stroke the soft hair on his forearms, feel the bristles on his chin brush against her cheek. All she had to do was touch his sleeve to feel the firm muscles beneath the thin fabric.

Good Lord.

If she did not calm her rampant imagination, she was liable to swoon.

This would not do.

Lifting her chin, she stared into eyes that were remarkably blue. "I find I like your relaxed demeanour, my lord. The barriers of conformity can often make one appear cold and distant. A more personable approach allows one to glimpse the man beneath the complex layers of responsibility."

His eyes sparkled with amusement. "I am pleased you approve, Miss Roxbury." He turned to Mr Dempsey. "Now you are confident I am alive and well, I trust you will stay for dinner."

"Dinner? Surely you do not expect us to travel anywhere this evening?" Mr Dempsey frowned. "No. We thought to stay for a few days. That is if it's no trouble."

"A few days?" Lord Harwood gulped. Panic flashed in his beguiling eyes. His pallor turned grey, ashen. "A few days," he repeated. "Can … can you spare the time?"

"Of course." Mr Dempsey paused and narrowed his gaze. "Though it is apparent you do not find the thought of visitors at all appealing."

Lord Harwood glanced at her briefly. "I'm afraid I shall not be good company. As you can see, I have far too much work to—"

"You need to eat," Helena said. "We will be grateful to spend a few hours with you during mealtimes, converse over breakfast."

"I eat while working."

"You eat while working?" Helena asked.

"It saves time."

"I hardly see how that is productive," Mr Dempsey countered. "I would find it a distraction."

Sarah looked to the floor. The tension in the air was stifling. It was obvious Lord Harwood wished to be left alone in peace and she was not so desperate as to force her company on anyone.

"I believe I shall take my leave." Sarah straightened. Humiliation had given way to annoyance. "This conversation calls for privacy and so I shall wait outside."

At the first opportunity, she would request to be conveyed to Hagley Manor. When accepting Mr Dempsey's proposal, she had expected the visit to last somewhat longer than ten minutes.

"Please wait, Miss Roxbury," Helena said. "We are so used to speaking openly we forget ourselves in front of guests. I am certain Lord Harwood meant nothing by his reluctance to offer his hospitality. Indeed, why would a gentleman not wish to be in the company of those who care for him?"

"Unless he has something to hide," Mr Dempsey added.

"What could I possibly have to hide?" Lord Harwood brushed his hand through his hair and gave a heavy sigh. "I am a gentleman who likes to plan for every eventuality. I see nothing wrong with that. Arriving without notice unsettles my equilibrium." He turned to Sarah. "Please, Miss Roxbury, I insist you stay. Indeed, if you will excuse me, I shall go and change my clothes. Chadwick will arrange for tea to be served in the drawing room and I will join you momentarily."

"Well, my lord, I would not decline the opportunity of a bed for the evening," Sarah said, though was a little baffled by the lord's sudden intake of breath. "But you must be left to your work. In the morning, I shall make arrangements to return to Hagley Manor."

True to form, conflicting emotions marred Lord Harwood's face: she saw instant relief though the corners of his mouth took a downward turn and his gaze grew distant.

"Then I shall spend the rest of the day attending to your needs." Lord Harwood blinked and swallowed deeply. "What I mean is I shall ensure your stay is a pleasurable one." He moved to the other side of his desk, opened the top drawer and swept the papers inside before locking it and removing the key. "Indeed, I shall not think of work for the rest of the day."

"It is more than you have been able to manage of late," Mr Dempsey said bluntly.

Sarah studied the viscount with interest. The faint dark circles under his eyes, accompanied by tight shoulders and a rigid jaw, did not suggest a preoccupation with work. She would wager he had not slept. What could be so pressing a problem it would keep a gentleman of his wealth and status awake at night?

Indeed, for the first time since making his acquaintance, she knew there was something dreadfully wrong.

He was a man of meticulous standards, approached every situation with care and thought. Work was obviously important to him. So why had he shoved the papers into the drawer as though they were nought but ink-stained mistakes ready for the basket? And if he chose to treat his documents with such disrespect why lock them away like priceless jewels?

Mr Dempsey was right.

Lord Harwood was hiding something. His secret had forced him to withdraw from Society. It had forced him to distance himself from those who loved him.

But what unfortunate event would make him feel he must shoulder the burden alone?

CHAPTER 6

*I*t took every ounce of strength Anthony possessed not to sprint from the room in a state of panic.

Good Lord. How the hell was he supposed to entertain family when they had no notion he was guardian to a six-month-old baby? There would be questions. Too many for him to contemplate. He would be forced to tell them about Emily, and then God knows what Lucas would do.

If that was not enough to contend with, temptation would be but a few feet away from his bedchamber, her curvaceous form sprawled seductively on top of his soft sheets. Once asleep, her peaceful sighs would drift through the corridors, calling to him like a siren's song, luring him from the safety of his chamber down into the depths of her welcoming body.

I would not decline the opportunity of a bed for the evening.

That one innocent comment had set his body aflame. Did the lady not know what she did to him? Did she not know his control was held together by nothing more than a silk thread?

He paused on the landing, cursed and punched the air.

What the blazes was Lucas thinking, bringing Sarah

Roxbury to Elton Park? As family, his brother and sister-in-law were hardly considered appropriate chaperones. Perhaps they did not realise they would be called upon to protect the lady's virginity as well as her reputation.

His mind chose that moment to conjure a vivid, rather erotic image of him thrusting past the problem.

Bloody hell!

Was there to be no end to his torment?

Anthony stopped on the landing to catch his breath. He would need full use of his faculties if he hoped to prevent them from discovering the truth.

It would be an impossible task. His problems were insurmountable.

After all, he was now a guardian, a lord framed for murder, a victim of extortion and a man so riddled with desire it consumed his every waking thought.

Shaking his head to clear his mind, Anthony tapped gently on the door to the nursery.

Mrs Russell opened it a mere inch and peered out. "Are you alone, my lord?"

"I am, for the moment."

The woman stepped back for him to enter and then eased the door gently until it clicked shut. "Mrs Adams informed me you have visitors. She explained the need for privacy."

Despite whispering, the woman had a harsh edge to her tone. With her fiery red hair scraped back into a severe knot, coupled with her stern features, he suspected she had the ability to make others do her bidding regardless of their complaint.

"My brother has arrived unexpectedly. I am not in a position to inform him of the new addition to the family. Hence I will need your full cooperation to ensure the child remains undiscovered."

Mrs Russell looked down her pointed nose, her disdain for secrecy and deceit evident. "What is it you would have me do, my lord?"

Do? What the hell was he to do?

"I shall need you to go out for a few hours." Anthony kept his arms at his sides for fear of flapping about like a distressed hen.

"And where would you like us to go?" Mrs Russell replied calmly.

Go? Damn it. Could the woman not think for herself?

"Erm … Carter will convey you to Witham. You are to take William and spend the rest of the day there. I will of course cover any expenses incurred. We will dine at eight this evening, during which time you will return and settle the boy in his crib."

Mrs Russell stared at him. "I have no objection to an outing, my lord. On the contrary, I believe fresh air will do the child the power of good, but—"

"But what, Mrs Russell? You think I should be honest? You think it is too long to keep a child outdoors?" He did not have time to dillydally. "Know you are free to speak."

Mrs Russell raised a brow. "I would not presume to offer advice to a gentleman of your standing, my lord, but I have found the truth always serves one well. I doubt your brother will take offence at not being told about your ward."

"The truth is not an option," he replied bluntly. A murderer lurked in the shadows, a man with the power and position to ruin lives. Deceit was the price of protection.

"Then I shall adhere to your orders, my lord, but what am I to do tomorrow? To take the child out continuously for long periods would be considered detrimental to his health."

Tomorrow? Lord, he just wanted to make it to the end of the day.

"I will find a way to shorten their visit," he said, though he felt a sharp pang in his chest at the thought of being rude to Miss Roxbury. Anthony dragged his hand down his face. "For the time being, we should focus our attention on making it till morning, free from discovery."

Mrs Russell sighed. "Then I shall say a prayer, my lord, as we are sure to need an element of divine intervention."

After attending to his unkempt demeanour and joining his guests to take tea in the drawing room, Anthony was just starting to relax when Mrs Adams entered to inform him the rooms were prepared and ready.

For fear of what Lucas might find should he go snooping about upstairs, Anthony escorted them to their bedchambers so they could rest and change before dinner.

"I'm afraid your old room has a touch of damp and so this room should suffice," Anthony said, directing Lucas and Helena to a bedchamber in the west wing overlooking the garden, a room far enough away from the nursery. "A man is coming down from Terling to assess the damage. He advised against occupants for the time being." Anthony opened the door, and they followed him inside. "As you know this room has the best view of the grounds."

Lucas turned his nose up at the papered walls and soft furnishings. "Did you not know I have an aversion to peacocks? I cannot quite fathom why someone would want to lie in bed at night and stare at rows of beady eyes and pointed beaks. In my opinion, royal blue and green make for a ghastly combination."

"With so many birds on the wall it is difficult to know where to focus one's eye," Miss Roxbury said, lingering in the doorway.

"I quite like the wallpaper. It gives the room an exotic, Oriental feel." Helena walked over to the window and looked out over the garden. Her smile faded as she turned around. "But what of George? Is the nursery not at the end of the hallway?"

Anthony cleared his throat. "Mrs Adams took the liberty of placing him in the room next door."

"Next door?" Lucas jerked his head. "But he has Miss Davis with him."

Lucas did not need to offer an explanation. While the staff were party to many conversations, he suspected his brother preferred an element of privacy and freedom in his bedchamber. As Anthony was a man with no need to consider the possibility of romantic interludes, it was an oversight on his part.

Helena sighed. "Oh, but George loves it in the nursery. The room is so light and airy, and he is stable enough to sit on the rocking horse." She strode purposefully over to the door. "Come. I'm sure it is not that far."

Heavens. Why could they not simply accept his decision?

With some reluctance, Anthony followed them to the nursery.

Lucas stopped outside, cast a mischievous smile and narrowed his gaze. "Are you going to tell me this room is damp, too?"

"Of course not." Anthony said a silent prayer as Lucas opened the door. While Mrs Russell had left the house with William, he had not thought to ask her to clear away the child's belongings.

As he stepped inside, Anthony scanned the floor, the rocking chair, every surface, looking for anything that might indicate there was a baby living in the house. With a deep sense of relief, he made a mental note to thank Mrs Russell for her foresight in cleaning the room.

"I have many happy memories of this room," Lucas

mused. He patted the rocking horse as though he had forgotten it was made out of wood, picked up the carved dove from the sideboard and examined it. "Mother would often sneak in and listen to us regale the story of Noah and his ark. I spent hours contemplating how on earth the poor man would find beds for all the animals."

Helena hugged her husband's arm. "Is that why you spend so much time in the nursery at home?"

"I enjoy playing with my son. But if I could sit on the rocking horse without breaking it, I would."

They all laughed although amusement was not an emotion that came easily to Anthony under present circumstances. He took a moment to watch Miss Roxbury. She stood over the crib, rocked it back and forth, ran her hand over the clean white sheets: a soft, gentle caress that conveyed the wealth of love she had to give.

It did not take much for him to imagine her with a child of her own. It took no effort at all for him to imagine bedding her repeatedly to fulfil his part of the task.

Heaven help him. She had no idea how much he wanted her.

"Ask Mrs Adams to move George and Miss Davis into the nursery," Lucas said. "They will be far more comfortable in here. Unless it would prove to be a problem."

"It will be no problem at all. I shall ask her to see to it at once." Damn it all. He could not refuse. When Lucas placed the dove back on the ark, Anthony added, "Perhaps you might prefer to sleep in here yourself. I was not aware of your fondness for wooden toys."

"It is often the simple things that give us the greatest plea-sure," Lucas replied with a smirk.

"Lucas is quite skilled with his hands," Helena said. "When he is not redesigning the garden, he often carves toys for George." She turned to Miss Roxbury. "Our son likes the soldiers and plays with them for hours, but I find the dragon to be his best work. It is a far more complicated design to conquer. It can seem an impossible task at times, but the pleasure gleaned is more than worth the effort."

For a reason that was quite beyond him, a faint blush touched Miss Roxbury's cheeks. "Then I feel I must take a lesson in perseverance," she said. "I find the slightest upset tends to sway me from my task."

"Take heart," Lucas said. "It took the dove but three attempts before it came back to bring Noah hope and signal an end to his suffering."

Miss Roxbury smiled and Anthony felt robbed of breath. She turned to face him. "Would you mind showing me to my room, my lord? I am somewhat weary after the day's travelling."

Anthony inclined his head. "Certainly. We shall leave my brother to play with his toys."

Finding Miss Roxbury a bed for the night proved to be as complicated as a mathematical puzzle. She could not sleep too close to the nursery for obvious reasons. Nor had he imagined putting her near his nephew, assuming he would have slept in the room initially allocated.

That left the rooms in the vicinity of his bedchamber.

To lie in bed at night and know Miss Roxbury lay but a few feet across the corridor was more than his weak heart could bear. For reasons he did not dare to explore, he wanted to impress her. The need to please her meant there was but one suitable room.

Gesturing to a door on his right, he said, "The bedchamber is small, but I believe rather quaint. I hope it will be adequate for your needs."

He followed her into the room, tugged discreetly on his

ADELE CLEE

cravat for it suddenly felt too warm for his liking. Though he knew the white and gilt decor was innately feminine, he had not anticipated his body's reaction to seeing her in the intimate space.

She examined the paintings on the wall panels: pictures of Venus and Cupid, inspired by Raphael. She ran her hands over the gold silk covering the chair. He watched, dumbstruck, imagined ushering her back out into the corridor in the hope of recapturing her initial look of wonder.

Miss Roxbury swung around to face him, her eyes dancing with delight. "It is so beautiful, my lord. I can hardly catch my breath."

She was beautiful. Rare. Unique. Utterly captivating.

The muscles in his abdomen grew uncomfortably tight. "I am pleased you approve." Good Lord. His tongue felt thick in his throat. His voice sounded an octave higher, a little croaky.

"Approve? I am spellbound. You do know you will have to find a way to entice me out of here." She placed her palm on her stomach. "Not even the prospect of dinner could persuade me otherwise."

"While it took some thought to find the perfect room, I would have made you sleep in the scullery had I anticipated your reluctance to leave."

She pursed her lips, the look too coy to bestow upon a man near the brink of losing control. "And what factors did you consider when allocating me this room?"

Damn. The woman was far too forthright.

"My primary concern was your comfort." The lie fell easily from his lips. "And the room is sufficiently placed so you will not suffer any disturbance." That was the truth.

She raised a brow. An amusing smile played on her lips. "You mean you chose the room furthest away from your bedchamber."

"Temptation strikes the breast of even the most pious of men, Miss Roxbury." He could not prevent his gaze falling to her lips. "I would be a fool to consider myself immune to your charms."

Her gaze travelled slowly over him. "*Fool* is the last word I would use to describe you, my lord. I believe you know exactly what you are about."

She stepped forward, and he made no protest when she straightened the knot on his cravat, brushed dust from the shoulders of his clean coat. Nor did he step away when her palm fell to his chest and covered his heart.

Breathe, damn it.

Anthony closed his eyes in a bid to bolster his control. His other senses sprang to life. He could feel her breath breeze against his cheek. The sweet scent of orange blossom and jasmine enveloped him. With every breath she took, he could picture the rise and fall of creamy flesh.

"I believe you are a man of many secrets," she whispered, her mouth but a fraction from his ear. "I sense a battle raging inside and cannot help wondering what it would take for you to surrender."

She did not wait for his answer.

Without any warning, her lips touched his. Though the pressure was light, he felt desire shoot through his body at such speed it almost knocked him off his feet. Her mouth brushed against his once, twice, the third time merely to tease.

Before he had a chance to respond, she stepped back. He felt the loss instantly. Shaking himself awake from the blissful dream, Anthony opened his eyes.

Miss Roxbury smiled at him. The playful glint in her eye stoked the internal flames he was struggling to tame.

She walked serenely over to the door, hugged the edge in

such a way as to indicate it was time for him to leave. "I feel in need of a rest, my lord. I have another long journey to make on the morrow."

Anthony hovered on the threshold, relief obliterated by disappointment. "You intend to leave for Hagley Manor?"

"I do, my lord, unless I happen upon a reason to stay."

CHAPTER 7

*S*arah closed the bedchamber door and exhaled deeply. With her fingers still wrapped around the handle, she took a moment to calm her racing heart.

Kissing Anthony Dempsey had not proved to be a problem. But fighting the urge to throw her arms around his neck and plunder those sensuous lips was harder than she imagined. It was hardly the sort of kiss poets spent sleepless nights deliberating. But the action served to make her position clear.

She wanted more from him.

She wanted everything he had to give.

Some might say she was nought but a foolish girl, that she must be immune to the pain of rejection. Some might consider her efforts desperate. Pitiful.

But Sarah had seen the way he looked at her: with lust, with longing. In those unguarded moments, she glimpsed the true measure of the man. When her lips had touched his, she'd felt an intense passion raging through his rigid body. She sensed his angst, his inner turmoil.

At dinner, he wore the same anxious expression, hidden beneath a veil of feigned smiles and weak chuckles. Had she a sovereign for every time he glanced at the window, for every time he brushed his hand through his hair and sighed, well, she would have the funds to buy the grandest house in Mayfair.

Was he expecting someone?

Doubt crept in to weave its wickedness.

Perhaps he had a mistress. Perhaps his secrecy regarding the papers on his desk stemmed from a need to protect the identity of the lady behind the love notes.

No.

Anthony Dempsey was not a man to toy with a lady's affections. Honour flowed like blood through his veins. Integrity formed the basis of his every thought and deed.

When they moved into the drawing room, he seemed more at ease. So much so, his smile almost reached his eyes.

"Either your housekeeper has ordered too much port and had nowhere to store it," Mr Dempsey began, "or you are intent on plying me with alcohol until I can no longer stand."

Sitting with his legs crossed at the ankles, Lord Harwood raised his crystal glass in salute. "I thought you'd come here to relax and enjoy my company. I am simply extending my hospitality."

Mr Dempsey raised an arrogant brow. "Do I look like a man who needs an inducement to have a good time?"

"No. You look like a man who needs help to forget other people's troubles and to concentrate on his own."

Mr Dempsey appeared a little surprised by his brother's directness. "I am a man who does not need the courage gleaned from liquor to speak my mind. Perhaps it is you who needs a drink, for you fear hearing what it is I have to say."

"You have made your opinion quite clear on more than one occasion." Lord Harwood stood. He snatched the glass from Mr Dempsey's hand and refilled it at the drinks table. "Would you care for another sherry, Miss Roxbury?"

Already, she had been far too free with her emotions, far too brazen in her actions. While another glass would work to soothe her anxious spirit, she could not risk baring her heart and soul completely.

"No. Not for me."

"Helena, can I interest you in another tipple?"

Helena shook her head. "One drink is enough for me. I shall be asleep before my head touches the pillow."

Seated next to his wife on the sofa, Mr Dempsey leant closer and whispered in her ear. Helena smiled in response, her hand trembling a little as she placed her glass on the side table.

"Perhaps we should all retire for the evening." Mr Dempsey stood, stretched, did not bother to suppress a yawn. "I'm afraid five hours in a carriage has taken its toll. And I am not as nimble as I used to be."

"Oh, I don't know," Helena replied. "For a gentleman of your height and broad stature, I would say you're still quite flexible."

"Yes, but at my age it takes constant work."

Lord Harwood returned to the seating area and handed Mr Dempsey his drink. "Surely you're not abandoning me at such an early hour. I thought you objected to my constant need for solitude. Sit. Stay for a while. Tell me about the plans for your garden."

Mr Dempsey placed his port on the side table. "I am tired of sitting. I need to stretch my legs."

Lord Harwood turned to Sarah. "What about you, Miss Roxbury? Is it not too early for you to retire?"

"After spending an interesting few hours in my room, I am not at all tired, my lord." She heard the seductive lull in her voice that reflected her earlier mood. Being in Lord Harwood's company made her body react in a way no innocent lady should be able to comprehend.

"Are we the only ones who do not wish to end the night prematurely?" He walked over to the window, parted the drapes and peered up at the night sky. "There's an abundance of stars out this evening and not a cloud in sight. Perhaps we should take a stroll in the garden and examine the cosmos. We could try to determine which one of the bright lights is actually a planet."

Sarah jumped to her feet. She held on to the arm of the chair to steady her balance. "You would not mind?"

"Of course not." Lord Harwood smiled. "At this time of year, Saturn can be seen in the evening sky, though I believe it cannot be observed after midnight. Did you know it was Galileo who first noticed that the planet had rings?"

Knowledge was food for her soul. She hurried to the window. "No. But I know it takes its name from the god Saturnus of ancient Roman mythology."

He appeared impressed. "Saturnus," he mused, "the god of agriculture and wealth."

"And often thought of as the god of liberation. I imagine the feeling of freedom after a time of powerlessness is something to celebrate."

"Indeed." His gaze travelled over her face. The look in his eyes could best be described as *hungry*—hungry to hear her opinion, hungry for something else entirely. "In Rome, one may still witness the ruins of the Temple of Saturn."

"You have seen the ruins?"

"I have."

Sarah clutched her hands to her breast as it was the only way to contain her excitement. "Oh, I would love to visit such an ancient city." Romantic ideas flooded her mind. "When I marry, I would do everything in my power to persuade my husband to take me on our own *Grand Tour*. We'd go to Florence and Venice and Verona. Sit in the piazza and gaze upon the ancient wonders."

"I am overcome with excitement just listening to you," Helena said.

Sarah glanced briefly over her shoulder. She had forgotten about the Dempseys. "They are just the whimsical dreams of a country girl."

Lord Harwood swallowed visibly. "I am certain your husband will be more than happy to grant you whatever your heart desires." He gestured to the window. "But for now, perhaps you will be content to observe the wonders of nature, relish in a little celestial bliss."

Being with Lord Harwood proved heavenly in itself. Seeing pleasure warm his eyes, seeing a genuine smile touch his lips, made her want him all the more.

"Is the moon visible tonight?" she asked.

Lord Harwood stepped aside, held the drapes open and motioned for her to come closer to the window. "The moon is in its third quarter and casts a silvery sheen over the whole garden."

He was right. Tonight, the garden held a mystical, magical quality. It was the scene of fairy tales, a scene where even one's most fanciful ideas brimmed with possibility. It would provide the perfect opportunity for him to give her a reason to stay.

"If we are to venture outside, I will need to find something warmer to wear."

His gaze dipped to the neckline of her gown, drifted slowly back up the column of her throat. "I'll call Chadwick and have a maid bring whatever you need."

"Do not trouble Chadwick at this hour," Helena said. "It will take but a minute for us to find our jackets."

"Our jackets?" Mr Dempsey enquired. "You wish to examine the stars, too?"

"I wish to do anything that would give us a reason to walk outdoors."

"You will find a few new additions to the garden," Lord Harwood said. "There was a bankruptcy sale at Moseley Manor. I acquired three new statues."

Mr Dempsey turned to his wife and smiled. "Then you should hurry and find your jacket."

"Do you enjoy sculptures, Mr Dempsey?" Sarah said.

"I do, Miss Roxbury. I find there is something about carved stonework that puts a man in a pleasurable mood."

CHAPTER 8

They left the gentlemen to their drinks and had no sooner closed the door to the drawing room when Helena reached for Sarah's hands and held them tight.

"I must thank you," Helena whispered. "I have not seen Anthony look so happy in months."

Sarah shared Helena's excitement. When Lord Harwood smiled the whole world seemed a far more joyful place. "Mr Dempsey was right. The more time Lord Harwood spends in our company, the more relaxed he appears."

"It is the time he spends in your company that brings the biggest change in him."

Sarah desperately wanted to believe it was true. But at dinner, she had witnessed the evidence of the secret he carried. The weight of his problem caused his shoulders to slump, the corners of his mouth to sag.

"Despite his cheerful mood, something troubles him deeply," Sarah admitted. "If only he would speak up and ask for help."

Helena sighed. "As head of the family, he would never burden us with estate business. No. We must discover the root of the problem for ourselves." She looked back over her shoulder before continuing. "You must persuade him to confide in you."

Sarah pursed her lips. "I told him I am leaving in the morning unless he gives me a reason to stay."

Helena's eyes widened. "You did? That explains his desire to stroll about the garden. You have given him no option but to examine his feelings." She paused. "But surely you don't mean to leave?"

The heavy ache in her chest returned. "I have no choice now. I must be true to my word. If he does not—"

"Wait." Helena raised her hand. "Do you hear a noise?"

Sarah strained to listen. A faint whimpering echoed through the hall to pierce the silence. "It sounds like crying."

Helena shook her head. "It must be George. I should check on him. Perhaps the long carriage ride has made him restless this evening, and Miss Davis is struggling to settle him in his bed."

"I shall come with you."

Helena took the candlestick from the console table, but as they climbed the stairs, the sound faded into the distance. They stood outside the nursery, somewhat baffled.

Helena put her ear to the door. "All is quiet." She handed Sarah the candlestick and prised the door from the jamb, peered inside before making a hasty retreat. "It was too dark to be certain, but I believe both George and Miss Davis are asleep. How odd."

"You must have been mistaken. In a house this size one would expect strange noises at night." Indeed, in all old houses one heard weird creaks and groans.

"But you heard it, too."

"I heard something," Sarah said as they walked to the top

of the stairs. "Though it could have been nought but the wind howling through the servants' quarters."

"The wind? But the sky is clear, the night mild. Anthony would not have suggested walking outdoors had there been a chance of catching a chill." Helena narrowed her gaze. "No. It was definitely a child crying. As a mother, you develop an ear for such things."

"Perhaps one of the servants has a child. Lord Harwood strikes me as a loyal, compassionate gentleman, even to his staff. I could not imagine him turning a girl out for one stupid mistake." As soon as the words left Sarah's lips, a frisson of fear ran through her. "You do not think … think that is what is troubling the viscount. You do not think he has … has—"

"Of course not," Helena snapped, understanding Sarah's train of thought completely. "Anthony would never abuse his position in such a manner."

"I know." Sarah's sad sigh conveyed her remorse. The thought should not have even entered her head. "My mind concocts all sorts of silly stories in a bid to discover what ails him."

Helena straightened. "Well, there is only one way to put our minds to rest. We must investigate. At the very least, we will find it is nothing at all and can spend the next hour laughing about our overactive imaginations."

"It is *your* overactive imagination," Sarah whispered with amusement as they descended the stairs to the hall. "I said it was the wind."

They followed the corridor leading back to the dining room and opened the door halfway along which led to the servants' quarters. They had taken but three steps down the stone staircase when the high-pitched cry made them pause.

"I knew it." Helena's tone carried a hint of satisfaction.

"There is a baby. Come, the child sounds as though it is in pain."

Sarah gripped the metal handrail. "Do you think the baby belongs to a maid?"

"I cannot see what other explanation there can be."

Once at the bottom, they followed the anguished wails to a wooden door in the basement passage. It was so small a gentleman would have to stoop to enter.

"Do they presume servants are shorter than other folk?" Sarah whispered.

"These are the maids' rooms. Perhaps it is to deter disreputable houseguests from forcing unwarranted advances. In the dark, the rake would hit his head on the overmantel, his loud groan sure to wake the neighbours."

While Helena's comment proved amusing, Sarah knew such despicable behaviour was commonplace. Terrible things often happened below stairs. Indeed, the candle flame flickered as an icy chill breezed past them. It was as if the residual energy left after such a harrowing event still lingered in the corridors.

"It is so cold down here." Sarah held the candlestick steady despite shivering. "No wonder the child is crying."

Helena tapped the door twice. They could hear a woman singing soothing words, but she did not answer. The child quietened but then a shrill squeal shattered the lullaby's sweet melody.

"Perhaps she cradles the child and cannot come to the door." Helena wrapped her fingers around the handle. "We should see if we can help."

Sarah nodded.

They opened the door gently to find a woman pacing the floor, rocking a babe in her arms. She was not wearing the uniform of a housemaid. The simple grey dress was that of a governess or nursemaid. Her fiery red hair was scraped back in a knot. From her profile, she appeared too old to be the child's mother.

"Forgive the intrusion," Helena said as they stepped into the room. "But we heard the child crying and came to see if we could help."

The woman swung round, her wide eyes revealing fear as opposed to shock. "I … I did not hear you come in." Her frantic gaze scanned their attire. "Forgive me, madam. Please, do not trouble yourself."

Sarah offered a reassuring smile. "Can we help in any way?"

The woman shook her head. "He is cutting his first tooth and will not settle."

Helena stepped forward and touched the babe's head, pressed the back of her fingers gently to his cheeks. "He feels a little hot. Have you given him anything? Does he have a teether, something hard to bite down on?"

"I've tried a lump of sugar wrapped in a cloth. I've tried a paste of honey and brandy."

"I have two younger sisters," Sarah said. "Our nursemaid gave them cold, washed carrots to bite. If the child pulled at the ear, she would rub the cheeks in a circular motion." She placed the candlestick on top of the dark oak chest of drawers. "Can I hold him for a moment?"

The woman appeared hesitant, but it was obvious she welcomed the offer of assistance.

Sarah took the child in her arms. His cheeks glowed berry red. The skin was dry where he had rubbed against his blanket to bring comfort. She stroked the babe's head, observed the quality of his nightgown.

The boy was not the child of a servant.

Piecing together the relevant clues: Lord Harwood's

reluctance to place his nephew in the nursery, his lack of enthusiasm for visitors, his anxiety, it was clear this was the problem weighing on his mind.

Lord Harwood's relationship to the child was the question currently plaguing Sarah's thoughts. But despite evidence to the contrary, she had trust in his integrity. She was confident he would provide a reasonable explanation.

"The child should be in the nursery. I do not know what possessed Lord Harwood to hide him away from us down here." Sarah knew to choose her words carefully if she had any hope of dragging the truth from the woman. "I do not know why he insists on secrecy."

"I agree," Helena said. "Surely he knows we would support his effort to care for those in need."

The woman shook her head. "You cannot blame his lordship. Under the circumstances, he has tried his best."

The child let out a heart-wrenching cry. Sarah rocked him, put the tip of her finger in his mouth and let him bite down. "We must find you a bedchamber upstairs. There is to be no more deceit. I know he did what he thought was right, but I am just glad we have discovered the truth."

Helena came to stand at Sarah's side. "And what are we to call the latest edition to the family?"

"The boy's name is William, madam."

"What a lovely name," Helena said. "While Lord Harwood has not divulged the nature of his relationship to the boy, I must assume the child is … is illegitimate."

Helena spoke calmly, yet Sarah's heart pounded wildly in her chest. She held her breath whilst she waited for the answer.

The woman raised a reproachful brow. "His lordship is a gentleman of honour. The child is not illegitimate. The child is his ward."

Helena sighed. "Well, thank goodness you told me, Mrs …"

"Mrs Russell."

"Thank you, Mrs Russell. It would have been awfully embarrassing had I jumped to conclusions. Now, you must go to Mrs Adams and tell her to find a suitable bedchamber for the evening. And tomorrow you may move back into the nursery."

Mrs Russell's mouth opened and closed numerous times. Eventually she gulped. "But I cannot go against his lordship's wishes."

"Have no fear. I shall inform Lord Harwood of the arrangements. We shall take William with us whilst you prepare the room."

Mrs Russell inclined her head for how could the woman protest?

Accompanied by Helena, Sarah carried the babe upstairs to the drawing room. The motion seemed to settle him, or perhaps the change in scenery proved to be a distraction.

They entered the room to find Lord Harwood gazing out of the window. Mr Dempsey stood in front of the fire with his hands clasped behind his back.

"How long does it take to find a jacket?" Lord Harwood said as he swung around to greet them. The smile touching his lips faded. His face took on a deathly pallor.

Mr Dempsey narrowed his gaze. "What have we here?"

"In our haste to find our jackets we seem to have stumbled upon something far more interesting," Helena said with a look of curious enquiry.

"You found a child whilst wandering the corridors?" Mr Dempsey asked incredulously.

"We did." Sarah placed a kiss on the boy's forehead. "This is William, Lord Harwood's ward."

CHAPTER 9

A deafening silence filled the room. They all stared at him, eyes wide and lips thinned, waiting for his response. Shock robbed him of the ability to speak. Fear rendered him rooted to the spot. The chaotic ramblings in his mind made it difficult to hear his inner voice.

"Your ward?" Deep furrows appeared between Lucas' brows. He shook his head numerous times. "What on earth are they talking about? We have no family or friends who would ask such a thing of you."

Anthony struggled to focus, his gaze flitting to a nondescript point on the far wall.

An innocent walk to find their jackets had resulted in them discovering his secret. It was only one part of the problem—the smallest most insignificant part if truth be told. Whatever happened from hereon in, Lucas could not discover the full extent of Anthony's misfortune.

With a heavy sense of sorrow in his heart, he met Miss Roxbury's gaze. Damn, she was beautiful. Even more alluring whilst holding the child in her arms. The corners of her mouth curled up into a reassuring smile. It was a gift from the gods. Her nod of reassurance gave him the courage to speak up and defend his decision.

"William has been my ward for the last five months." Anthony swallowed down the hard lump in his throat. He would have to tell them more than that. "The responsibility was thrust upon me. It was not something I chose to undertake."

Lucas jerked his head back. "You've been the child's guardian for five months, and you did not mention the fact to your family?"

"It was not a decision—"

"To whom does the child belong?" Lucas interrupted. "Where are his parents?"

Helena gripped Lucas' arm. "Can you not give him a moment to speak?"

William let out a sudden shriek, and Miss Roxbury paced back and forth to settle him. She whispered soothing words, held him close to her breast. Anthony sighed. God, how he wished for peace and comfort, too.

"I need a drink." With his mind a jumbled mess, Anthony refilled his glass, flopped down into the chair and stared up at the figures towering over him like judges on the bench at the Bailey.

Deceit was his only crime, and perhaps stupidity.

Lucas and Helena sat on the sofa whilst Miss Roxbury continued to pace the floor in her efforts to reassure the child.

"In your own time," Helena began, "tell us how you came by such a huge responsibility."

Anthony swallowed a mouthful of brandy. Thankfully, the spirit proved to be far more potent than port. "The story is long, and so you must bear with me. It is best I start at the beginning."

"Well, that would be helpful," Lucas sneered.

Anthony was not offended by his brother's clipped tone. Lucas often used sarcasm to disguise his injured pride.

"When my gamekeeper, Harold Compton, passed away two years ago he left a daughter. She was twenty-four, had worked on the estate and never married. Consequently, I continued to let her live in the cottage, rent-free, until she was of a mind to find a husband."

Lucas sat forward. "You speak of Emily Compton?"

The mere mention of her name brought the horrific images flooding back: the blood, far too much blood, the white skin, the lifeless eyes. It was not the sort of death he would wish on an enemy, let alone a woman he'd known for most of his life. Lucas knew of his attachment to the girl. Anthony prayed he would be tactful when speaking in front of Miss Roxbury.

"We spent time together as children. Had our parents known, it would have been forbidden. Her mother died when she was just a babe." History had seen fit to repeat itself. "The servants here took care of her, and so we spent many summers roaming the woods, climbing trees, doing what all children do when raised in the country. It is not a secret I developed an affection for her. A young man is easily won over by a warm smile and mild flattery."

"Hence the reason you ignored all notion of propriety and let her continue living on the estate," Lucas mocked.

"What I thought was a romantic affection proved to be the platonic feelings of friendship." It was important Miss Roxbury knew no other woman had staked a claim on his heart. "What would you have had me do? Throw her out onto the street? I refused to see her alone and destitute."

"There are rooms downstairs."

"The cottage has been her home for more than twenty years."

Sarah Roxbury met his gaze. Only one emotion was evident in her pretty blue eyes: compassion. "You have a generous heart, my lord. There is no shame in that."

"There is but a hair's breadth between generosity and foolishness, Miss Roxbury, but your faith in my character is touching."

Lucas cleared his throat. "Has Emily fallen on hard times? Is she the child's mother? Have you taken him in to help support her?"

Anthony pushed his hand through his hair and rubbed the back of his neck to ease the mounting tension in his muscles. "Yes. William is Emily's child, but the arrangement is not temporary." He swallowed deeply, expecting a sudden lurch in his stomach when he spoke again. "I'm afraid to say Emily is dead."

Helena gasped and clutched Lucas' arm tight.

Miss Roxbury cradled the child, closed her eyes and kissed his forehead.

Anthony felt numb.

"Forgive me," Lucas said. "I did not know. I trust it was not a painful, prolonged illness."

What the hell was he supposed to say now?

To be vague about the events might give him more time to decide how to proceed, but it was too serious a subject to lie.

He looked to Miss Roxbury hoping to find the strength to continue. What he would give to be his ward. How wonderful it would feel to be oblivious to the pain, the horror, to be held in Miss Roxbury's warm arms until all his troubles melted away.

"The precise nature of her last moments is not a topic to discuss in the presence of ladies." Anthony exhaled deeply.

There was a moment of stunned silence. Perhaps they

were trying to determine his meaning. Perhaps they were imagining a range of ghastly possibilities.

"Am I interpreting your meaning correctly?" Lucas shuffled uncomfortably. He placed his hand over Helena's as though the gesture would protect her from the pain of the truth. "Are you saying her death was a result of … of criminal activity?"

Anthony could not form the words and so simply nodded.

Perhaps the room was deficient of air, for they all inhaled far too quickly as the significance of Anthony's silence penetrated.

Miss Roxbury stood still, her eyes glazed and distant. The gentle rap on the door made her jump.

Grateful for the distraction, Anthony bid the caller to enter.

Mrs Russell appeared. Despite a solemn countenance, she gave a weak smile. "The bedchamber is ready, my lord. The ladies insisted William find a more suitable place to sleep."

"William can move back into the nursery in the morning," Helena instructed in the confident, organised way he had grown accustomed. "It is far too cold for him in the basement."

Anthony had neither the strength nor the inclination to defend his earlier decision. "Of course."

Mrs Russell scooped the child from Sarah Roxbury's warm embrace.

"He is asleep for the moment," Miss Roxbury said, her tone brimming with kindness and affection. "I only pray you get some rest."

"Thank you." Mrs Russell inclined her head and left the room.

Anthony watched Miss Roxbury. Without the babe in her arms, she appeared lost, vulnerable.

"Perhaps I should leave, too." She clasped her hands in front of her, fiddled with her fingers. "Such a private conversation should not be shared with guests."

"Nonsense." Anthony stood and gestured to the chair. "I want you to stay. I owe you an explanation for the rather odd behaviour you have witnessed of late."

Her gaze flitted between his outstretched hand and the tapestry seat covering.

"Please, Miss Roxbury," Anthony continued. "It is important you know the truth." Or as much of the truth as he was willing to share. To hear everything would place her at unnecessary risk.

"Then I will stay. Know I will not breathe a word to anyone." She sat demurely. "You may trust me, my lord. I want nothing more than to help ease your burden."

His heart thumped wildly at the prospect of her doing just that. "Then take comfort that your presence here makes life's trials and tribulations more tolerable." Their gazes locked and he wished he was free to pursue his attraction.

"Do you know who is responsible for the crime committed against Emily Compton?" Lucas asked, the harsh element to his tone conveyed an urgent need to be apprised of the facts.

To know that would bring an end to his nightmare. Indeed, he would make the scoundrel pay dearly.

"The answer is yes and no," Anthony answered cryptically. "Again, I will attempt to explain the events in a logical order." He took his glass from the side table and downed the contents. The liquid fire trickled down his throat to relax his tight muscles. "Early last year, I held a small house party. Nothing elaborate, just a few gentlemen over to play billiards and cards. Well, I say a few, but there were five in attendance."

It took just a brief pause for breath for Lucas to make the obvious calculation. "Are we to assume one of these so called gentlemen took advantage of an innocent girl and consequently fathered Emily's child?"

"Oh, one of them is William's father." One of them had committed murder and resorted to blackmail. "But Emily was far from innocent. She wanted a wealthy husband. Those of us brought up in Society know the unwritten rules when it comes to affairs of a more licentious nature."

Helena sighed. "As a girl bred in the country, no doubt Emily was naive when it came to her expectations."

"Extremely naive. She thought their secret meetings romantic. She thought all men were possessed of loyalty and honour when it came to matters of the heart."

A pang of guilt forced him to look at Miss Roxbury. His determination to keep her safely at arm's length whilst still dallying with her affections could easily be construed as disrespectful.

Miss Roxbury met his gaze. "Why would she think any different when she had spent a lifetime in your company, my lord?"

The flattering remark went some way to soothe his conscience.

Lucas rubbed the back of his neck. "Then surely you must know the identity of Emily's lover. What are the names of the gentlemen who attended your party? Am I acquainted with any of them?"

"Does it matter?"

"Of course it matters. To pass pleasantries with such a man will make me seem weak. He will assume I am aware of the situation and that I approve of his disreputable behaviour."

Disreputable was far too tame a word for a man capable of taking a woman's life. If he told Lucas, his brother would insist on conducting his own investigation, one that involved fists not logic.

Anthony shook his head. "I cannot divulge their names until I have more information."

"More information," Lucas repeated incredulously. "And how do you suppose to gain any insight when the only person in possession of the facts is dead?"

"I am a little confused," Miss Roxbury said. "You said Emily died as a result of criminal activity. What exactly do you mean?"

The corners of Helena's mouth curled downwards. "He means she was killed by the hands of another, I suspect by her lover in a bid to keep his identity a secret."

The colour drained from Miss Roxbury's face. She put her hand to her throat. "I see."

"Though why such a thing was necessary is somewhat baffling," Helena added. "Miss Compton was hardly in a position to cause any mischief."

"Was there a funeral?" Lucas enquired coldly. "Did you not consider the possibility that I would have liked to attend?"

Bloody hell!

The story was about to become far more confounding.

"You need a body to have a funeral," he said, although that was not entirely true. He did not wait for them to bombard him with even more questions. "I shall come straight to the point for fear of causing confusion. I was the one who found her body. She was lying on the bed in the cottage. William was in his cradle, barely a month old, crying so fiercely his face was puffy and red. After taking a minute to compose myself, I brought the child to the house, before returning to assess the situation. Of course, I intended to inform the magistrate. But upon my return, I found the cottage empty."

They all stared at him as though he was a prime candidate for Bedlam and they were deliberating the best way to have him committed.

"The dead do not walk," Lucas said.

"I am aware of that." Anthony cast his brother a look of reproach. "The cottage is situated next to the lane. I heard horses' hooves pounding the dirt, ran outside to see an unmarked carriage rattling away. I chased after it until my chest burned, until I watched it disappear into the distance."

"You think the gentleman removed Emily's body to hide the evidence?" Helena asked.

"The coverlet was missing." Anthony pictured the macabre scene. "A trail of blood led from the bed all the way to the front door. I spent day and night walking the lanes, searching every ditch, every piece of woodland. I've had the boards up in the cottage, and therefore all the evidence leads me to conclude that her body was transported away from here in the carriage."

The blackmailer had since confirmed his suspicion, had also confirmed he possessed the only piece of evidence to incriminate Anthony in the crime.

"And with your mind plagued by fear and worry, you never thought to approach me?" Lucas' sombre tone stabbed at Anthony's heart. "Did it not occur to you that I could be of some help?"

"Lucas, I would trust you with my life. But you have a wife and a child, another on the way. After what happened with Lord Banbury, you cannot afford to be embroiled in another scandal."

"I am not a child, Anthony. I deserved the right to make that choice for myself."

Helena tutted. "Oh, for heaven's sake, Lucas. He didn't ask for our help because he was trying to protect us. He has carried the burden alone, with no one to support him, no one to help ease his fears. It breaks my heart to think of us laughing and joking while his mind was tormented by this terrible thing."

"If I may say," Sarah Roxbury began, "there is no point dwelling on what should have been. Lord Harwood desired secrecy, and so we must respect that it was a difficult decision for him to make."

For the third time this evening, Miss Roxbury had come to his defence. Anthony did not deserve her good opinion. He wished that he could show his gratitude for her continued support. He wished she would wrap her arms around him, gaze into his eyes and make him believe all would be well again.

"And so what now?" Lucas dragged his hand down his face and sighed.

"What do you mean?"

"You cannot sit here and do nothing. You must discover who is responsible and hold them to account. William has a father. He must sign over legal guardianship if you intend to care for the boy."

It was not as easy as Lucas believed. A step in the wrong direction would ruin their family name for generations to come. A hundred years from now, people would still regale the story of the mad viscount who murdered the gamekeeper's daughter.

"When you arrived, I was trying to formulate a plan. I thought a few discreet enquiries might lead me to rule out one or two gentlemen."

Lucas shuffled to the edge of the chair. "When everyone thought me a scoundrel, a dissolute rake and a rogue, you supported me. Without you and Helena I dread to think where I might be. Let me help you, Anthony. Let me at least be the person you confide in during your darkest hours. Trust me. Have faith that we will sort out this mess, so you may be free to move forward with your life."

"You are not in this alone," Helena added. "We are all here for you. Aren't we, Miss Roxbury?"

Miss Roxbury's eyes brimmed with an emotion he could not define. "You may count on me, my lord, to help in any way I can."

Anthony brushed his hand through his hair. "And what if it proves dangerous? What if reputations are ruined as a consequence?"

"The good opinion of a bunch of drunks and debauchers is of no importance to me," Lucas said. "I would rather go to my grave knowing I did right by my brother than to pander to prigs in the hope they speak well of me."

A chuckle burst from Helena's lips. "Forgive me. This is no laughing matter, but my husband has such a way with words."

"It's true," Lucas replied. "I have no love for those who parade about in Society like trussed-up pheasants."

"Well, you know my sentiment when I feel there has been a dreadful miscarriage of justice," Helena said, thrusting her chin in the air.

Anthony's heart felt lighter than it had in months. Damn it. He would not fail them. One way or another he would find a way to solve his problems.

"Then we are in this together." Anthony turned to Miss Roxbury. "I understand if you choose to leave. Indeed, should you require passage to Hagley Manor, my coachman will convey you there in the morning."

"That won't be necessary." She moistened her lips. "I believe you have given me ample reason to stay."

he gold tassels on the bed hangings flapped back and forth, caught in the gentle breeze drifting in through the open window of Sarah's bedchamber. There were thirty trimmings, all the same size, all moving in varying degrees. She had spent the last hour counting them, considered another attempt in the hope the monotonous ritual would make her drowsy.

But how could she close her eyes and slip into a peaceful slumber when all she could think of was Lord Harwood's terrible nightmares?

During his recount of the harrowing tale it had taken every ounce of strength she possessed not to hurry to his side, place a hand on his arm or smooth the lock of hair from his brow. Recalling the pain etched on his face as he spoke of Emily Compton's demise tore at her heart.

Yet some good had come from hearing his confession.

Now she knew the reason behind his reserved demeanour. Now she understood the discord between his clipped words and the desperate look of longing swimming in his blue eyes.

His sad story had opened the way for another startling revelation.

She was in love with him.

Why else would she make a fool of herself coming to Elton Park? Why else would she cling to the hope he might feel affection for her?

Oh, it was an impossible situation.

Frustration forced her from her bed. She paced back and forth, wringing her hands as a way to ease the mounting tension. What if he could not love her back? What if all he sought was a distraction from his troubles?

What would she do then?

She looked at the mound of plump pillows as other ladies would look at the latest dress designs from Paris. Sleep would elude her tonight unless she could divert her thoughts.

Glimpsing a brown leather-bound book on the side table, she picked it up. It had not been there earlier. The gold words embossed on the spine made her smile. It was Isaac Newton's book on astronomy. It could not be a coincidence. As she opened the cover, a small piece of paper floated to the floor.

Curiosity burned.

It was considered the height of rudeness to read another's personal missive. But she could not leave it lying there for a servant to find. All she had to do was slide the note back in between the leaves. Of course, she could not help but glance at the elegant script, could not help but notice her name scrawled boldly at the top.

Miss Roxbury,

I took the liberty of placing this book in your room. It is my gift to you. Like a rare and exotic flower, one's passion should be nurtured, given every chance to bloom into some-

thing magnificent. To know I might play a part in fulfilling but one of your dreams is more than I could ever hope for.

Yours,

Anthony Dempsey

The words washed over her like a warm, soothing wave. It was the most wonderful thing anyone had ever done for her. The thoughtful gesture caused hope to flare to life in her chest. With a little chuckle, she placed the precious piece of paper between the pages, twirled around and hugged the book tight. No doubt she would fall asleep still clutching it in her arms.

A sudden gust blew in through the gap between the ledge and the sash. The cool breeze brushed her bare ankles, sending a shiver shooting up her spine.

Placing the book on the bed, she hurried over to the window. She was about to push the sash down when she noticed a shadow moving through the formal gardens.

Anthony Dempsey stopped and bent his head to smell the roses. He hovered there for a moment before looking up at the inky canopy above, home to a glittering array of stars. Even from her elevated position, so far away, she sensed his disquiet. To her mind, his countenance conveyed sadness. It was there in the slow, ambling way he walked. It was there in the way his hand cupped the flower, how he savoured the scent as if it had a magical ability to bolster one's spirits. It was there in the way he pleaded to the heavens for an answer to his prayers.

Go to him.

The words lingered in a distant recess of her mind like a child clutching the door frame waiting for permission to enter. Despite trying to dismiss the idea, the words echoed again and again.

Go to him.

She couldn't. What would he think of her, parading around in the garden in her nightwear? What if someone saw them?

There is no one here to judge.

She couldn't. To be alone with him would prove too tempting for her weak heart to bear.

Sarah turned to walk away but stopped.

What if he needed to talk to someone? Such a heavy burden had the power to wear a man down until he was nought but dust on the ground.

If you love him why hesitate?

Without giving the matter another thought, she rummaged through the armoire looking for her travelling cloak. After throwing it around her shoulders and tying the ribbons, she pushed her feet into a pair of silk slippers and hurried out of the door.

He must have heard her racing along behind him on the gravel path.

"Miss Roxbury, is everything all right?" His wide eyes scanned her attire. "Has something happened? Is it the children?"

"No." The word was but a breathless pant. In her effort to reach the garden before he returned to the house, she had pushed herself too hard. "All ... all is well."

"Do you need to sit? Are you unwell?"

"No." She placed her hand on her chest. Her heart pounded against her palm. "I ... I saw you from my window and thought you might like company."

Whilst she believed honesty to be the best policy, it made her sound desperate.

"But it is late. You should be in your bed."

"So should you, my lord." The salacious implication to her words made her gasp. "I did not mean my bed. That was not an invitation."

The corners of his mouth curled up into a playful smile. "I am not so presumptuous to imagine it the case. Not unless Fate has plucked my dream from the air mid-flight."

There it was—as clear as a gentleman of his standing could allow.

Anthony Dempsey wanted her. Perhaps only in the physical sense but it was enough for now.

"I could not sleep," she confessed, resisting the urge to twirl her hair around her finger in the flirtatious way she had seen ladies do. Helena was right. To pretend to be anything other than herself was sheer folly. "I cannot stop thinking about what you said earlier. You have had such a lot to contend with."

"I did not intend to burden you with my problems." His gaze drifted over her hair tied loosely at the nape. Numerous strands whipped about in the breeze. "While I despise deceit, sometimes it is a necessary form of evil."

"Under the circumstances, I do not think anyone is in a position to judge." Indeed, when her parents died, Prudence had found the responsibility of raising her sisters more than challenging. "You did what you thought best. No one could argue with that."

Another shiver crept down her back. She wrapped her cloak tightly around her body for the cool night air penetrated the fine cotton of her nightgown.

"Your compassion does you credit, Miss Roxbury. But let me escort you back inside. It is far too cold to be out here in —" He waved his hand in the air, his chin almost touching his chest as he scanned her from head to toe.

"In my nightdress and travelling cloak."

"Indeed." He covered his mouth with his hand, craned his neck in a manner that suggested his valet had tied his cravat far too tightly.

There was something alluring about the odd glimpses of vulnerability he tried so desperately to hide. While she was by no means a woman of the world, it gave her confidence in her ability to please. Knowing she was out of doors in her nightclothes made her feel wicked and wanton.

"Let me walk with you awhile." She did not give him an opportunity to object, but stepped forward and placed her hand in the crook of his arm. "Tell me what troubles you so, that you would wander the garden alone at night."

Touching him caused the familiar tingling in her belly.

A chuckle escaped from his lips. The beautiful sound was like a potent elixir. She would make it her life's mission to hear his happiness radiate loud and hearty.

"You have an innate ability of making a statement sound like a request," he said. "You make it seem as though I have an option when clearly you are determined in your course."

"You can say no, my lord."

"I find the word *no* is not in my vocabulary when I am with you, Miss Roxbury."

"Excellent. Then you must walk with me until I can no longer keep my eyes open."

"If that is what you wish."

They walked to the end of the path in companionable silence. There was nothing like the incessant barrage of questions to elevate one's anxiety levels. The more time she spent in his company, the more her awareness of him grew. She did not need to gaze into his eyes to know the sadness consuming him minutes before had now subsided.

"Most ladies would refuse to walk out at night," he

suddenly said. "The activity is frowned upon. It is thought to lead to nought but a chill."

"Nought but trouble I dare say." If the warm feeling of desire flowing through her veins was of any consequence, trouble was less than an arm's length away. "There is something about the dark that lends itself to clandestine meetings. A fear of chills is instilled by one's governess or lady's maid simply to keep their charge safe."

"Is that so?" His amused tone led her to conclude he was smiling though she did not glance at his face. "Then I must assume either your governess was lacking in her responsibilities or you have a penchant for the clandestine."

There is nothing as alluring as the truth.

Mr Dempsey's words echoed in her ears. "My penchant has nothing to do with being secretive. Something else drew me out here tonight. I found I could not stay away."

"Then I must admit to experiencing similar feelings of late."

The path brought them to a crossroads. The statue in the centre looked like an awkward lump of grey stone in the dark.

"Which way now?" she asked, peering into the shadows.

"Left takes us to the orangery, right to the lawns." He pointed to all three paths as though she had no concept of direction. "If we continue ahead we have the option of the walled garden, the orchard, or the lake."

"How am I to choose? I am sure they are all equally inspiring." She imagined she would see nothing but black silhouettes and the outline of numerous grey shapes though she had no intention of spoiling the moment. The man at her side was the only thing of interest to her.

"I think the safest option is best," he said. "I find the dark leads one to be more adventurous. It allows for a certain freedom not exercised during the daylight."

She smiled in anticipation of teasing him. "You mean swimming in the lake under a blanket of stars is not on your list of recommended activities?"

He sucked in a deep breath. "Oh, there is nothing I would recommend more. But I fear such recklessness will prove dangerous in more ways than one."

"Then what would you say should I desire a midnight swim?"

Flirtatious banter proved to be entertaining.

"As I have already explained, I find I am reluctant to deny you anything, Miss Roxbury."

"Anything? Would you care to enlighten me as to what that might entail?"

He raised a brow. "The honourable part of my character demands I do not answer."

"Then you leave me no option but to use my imagination, my lord."

His heated gaze scorched her body. "Should your thoughts be in any way aligned with mine, Miss Roxbury, I am assured you will have a restless night's sleep."

Sarah laughed. She could spend a lifetime thinking of ways to tempt him. "Come. Then let us stroll around the lawn where we are not apt to be drawn to temptation."

A moment of silence ensued.

"Before we do, can I ask you to do something for me?"

Surely he must know she would do anything for him. "You know I will assist you in any way I can." It always felt good to come to the aid of others. When it came to Anthony Dempsey, she imagined philanthropy could become an obsession.

"I—" He stopped abruptly and sucked in a breath. "I want you to return to Hagley Manor in the morning."

It was as though someone had punched through her

ribcage, the broken and jagged bones piercing her heart. "You want me to leave?"

He dragged his hand down his face, struggled to look her in the eye. "I believe it will be for the best."

Mere moments ago they had laughed about frolicking in the moonlight. Now he did not want her near him.

"You do not want my help?" How the words tumbled from her lips was confounding, for the solid lump in her throat restricted her airways. "You do not want me to stay?"

He closed his eyes. Ragged breathing accompanied the heavy rise and fall of his chest: evidence of an internal battle raging.

She was forced to swallow deeply to stop the sudden surge of raw emotion. "You cannot keep doing this to me. You cannot keep pushing me away."

"This whole thing is a mess." He threw his hands in the air. "A woman was murdered on this estate. It is not safe here. Not until I find out who's responsible. If anything happened to you as a consequence of—"

"Nothing is going to happen to me." She closed the gap between them, placed her hand on his upper arm. "Let me stay."

"I cannot think clearly when I am around you." He stared into her eyes and gave a weary sigh. "I feel as though I am drowning in my own inadequacy. When I am with you like this, I cannot control myself."

"Then … then don't."

Pushing aside her fears, she stood on the tips of her toes and pressed her lips to his. It took less than a second for him to respond. His arm snaked around her back and pulled her tight to his muscular chest.

"Damn it. Why can I not say no to you?" he whispered as his mouth claimed hers.

CHAPTER 11

nthony could recall a few times in his life when he had felt helpless. The day his father shipped his brother off to Boston was perhaps one of the most memorable. Even so, he had never been at the total mercy of his emotions.

Sarah Roxbury held him captive. He was a slave to her wants and desires. Touching her brought an element of inner peace he had never known. Kissing her caused desire to rage through his body like a wildfire, consuming every rational thought, obliterating all notions of decency and decorum.

Driven by this wild need, he coaxed her lips apart, let his tongue penetrate the sweet depths of her mouth. Nothing prepared him for what it would be like to taste her. Nothing prepared him for the way his blood pumped too rapidly through his veins, the way it pooled and pulsed to tease and excite.

Her soft moan made his manhood swell. When her tongue brushed against his, it took all the strength he possessed not to lift her up so her thighs gripped his waist. Lord, how he wanted to push home and let everything else be damned.

"*Sarah.*" Her name breezed from his lips as he rained kisses along her jaw. The word confirmed he'd ignored all notions of logic and propriety.

"Tell me you want me," she whispered as she angled her head to offer him the elegant column of her throat. "Tell me you need me to stay."

He nipped at the sensitive part of her neck. God, he was so damn hungry for her, he feared he would never stop. But still, the words she wanted to hear were stuck in his throat.

Her delicate fingers travelled up under his coat. She fiddled with the buttons on his waistcoat until he felt the heat from her palms penetrate the fine lawn of his shirt. Those wicked hands caressed the muscles in his chest, scorching his skin until his mind became lost in a smoky haze.

"Tell me what is really in your heart," she muttered as her fingers crept around and down his back to draw him closer.

He found her mouth again, devoured her as though famished to the point of starvation. He had experienced lust, but never such an all-consuming passion. Never had he wanted to bed a woman so badly.

"*Anthony.*"

Lord help him. Hearing his name fall from her lips roused a primitive need to claim, to conquer, to care for and protect. Her natural essence enveloped him. It would be the only scent he craved whilst lying in his bed at night. The sweet, almost floral taste of her mouth promised a lifetime of wonderful tomorrows.

They broke again for breath.

"Tell … tell me the truth." Desire swam in her pretty blue eyes as she heaved to catch her breath. "You want me to stay. I can see it in your eyes. I can feel it in your touch. If you will not tell me, I shall be forced to discover the answer for myself."

The tips of her fingers brushed his hip, hesitated before brushing over the hard evidence of his arousal.

His head fell back, the sudden euphoria being too much for his weak body to bear. "Bloody hell. Do you not realise the effort it takes not to claim what I want? I want you more than I have wanted anything in my entire life."

A sensual smile graced her lips. "Then make me yours, Anthony. Do not fight it anymore."

"You do not know what you're asking." He had no choice but to look away for he was seconds from surrender.

"You cannot deny what exists between us." Her hands moved over his chest. Touching. Teasing. Tempting. It was as though she had the ability to be everywhere all at once. "You cannot keep pushing me away when that is not what you want."

"There is too much at stake." He could not be selfish. He could not ruin her for any other suitor should he fail in his mission. "When I have discovered the name of the man responsible for Emily's death, then I shall be free to move on with my life. As it stands, I know he is capable of murder. By associating with me, you would be putting yourself in a precarious position."

She shook her head. "What happened to Emily Compton was unfortunate, but it was obviously a crime of passion. There is no reason to assume I would be in any danger."

She was wrong, although he had to admire her determination. Indeed, it went some way to proving the depth of her affection.

"Perhaps initially it began as a lovers' quarrel," he agreed, "but now it has become a personal vendetta."

"A vendetta? A terrible thing has happened but do not make more of it than it is."

"There is more you do not know." He had to make her

understand though he knew to choose his words carefully. "The gentleman has since written to me. Numerous times. To taunt me. To remind me of my inadequacy." The burning need for revenge surfaced. God damn, he despised being taken for a fool. "Each time he writes he sends me a token, something symbolic, something he left on Emily's blood-stained pillow."

Miss Roxbury's eyes widened. "A token? What is it?"

"The gentleman sends me … he sends a small black feather."

Recognition dawned. She gasped, stepped back and covered her heart with her hand. "You mean to say … you mean—"

"The man who killed Emily is the same person who thrust the feather into your palm at Lord Daleforth's ball."

"But why?"

Anthony shrugged. "To let me know that he was watching me. It was a warning, a way of demonstrating his power. It was his way of letting me know he has the ability to ruin my life."

To speak of it brought him a modicum of relief. Giving the words in his head a voice confirmed he was not mad. This was not some horrid nightmare. The threats were real. His efforts to be rude and deceitful were justified.

Miss Roxbury stepped forward and placed her hand on his cheek. He closed his eyes briefly, took comfort from her tender touch. He was so damn tired he could rest his head in her lap and sleep for days.

"You should not have borne this problem alone. When we spoke earlier, none of us asked if you had reported the crime to the authorities. Am I correct in thinking you have not done so? Does the absence of a body make you fear suspicion will rest at your door?"

The lady was as intelligent as she was beautiful.

He clasped her hand, placed a light kiss on her palm. "In allowing Emily to live in the cottage, people will assume the child is mine," he said. Being kind was his only mistake. "They will believe I am the one responsible for her death. That I used my position to conceal a murder."

Miss Roxbury clutched his hand. "But when you tell them of the house party, when you give the names of the gentlemen in attendance, then that will surely cast doubt over your involvement."

She made it all sound so simple.

The truth clung to the tip of his tongue. It would take but a few spoken words to ease his burden.

"It would not make any difference."

"Of course it would," she persisted. "Many gentlemen would speak of your impeccable character. However, one of your five guests has a licentious past. I suspect this is not his first offence. A word in the ear of a gossip or two and I guarantee you'll discover his involvement in another scandal. It would be enough to shift suspicion."

Just tell her.

"It is more complicated than that."

"I do not see how."

"Some years ago, my brother was implicated in the murder of Lord Banbury. While he proved his innocence and caught the real culprit, people are still wary of his character. To have our family name linked to another murder will be disastrous for all of us."

"You are guilty of generosity. That is all." She clutched his hands and shook them as if to reinforce her point. "People will see that. There is nothing to implicate you in Emily's murder other than an act of kindness bestowed upon the daughter of a loyal servant."

Tell her.

"That is not entirely true. When I found Emily's body, I noticed a cane poking out from under the bed. But with William crying, I did not have the opportunity to pay it much attention." He spoke so quickly he was forced to suck in a breath. "It has since been made known to me that someone removed the cane from this house. The solid gold handle bears my family's crest, along with Emily's blood."

There was a moment of silence.

"I see." A frown marred her brow. "And where is this cane now?"

"When I returned to the cottage, it was gone. Should the item be presented with the body, it speaks as proof of my guilt." Indeed, it was part of the reason he had not hunted down every one of the guests and beaten them until they confessed.

Miss Roxbury dropped his hands and covered her mouth with her fingers.

Anthony searched her face, looking for a sign of doubt, looking for any indication she might suspect he had played a part in the crime. "Regardless of how it looks, you must know I had nothing to do with what happened to Emily."

Miss Roxbury snorted. "I would not be standing here with you in the garden at night were I not convinced of your innocence."

After the way he had behaved, he did not deserve her good opinion.

"But there is only one course of action to take," she continued. "You must do everything in your power to find the culprit. You must take back this item that incriminates you. For William's sake, you must discover what happened to Emily so you may lay his mother to rest."

Anthony exhaled deeply. While he acknowledged the truth in her words, the tasks seemed monumental.

"I don't even know where to begin. It would take months of planning. One wrong move or word and I could hang for a crime I did not commit." Panic flared. "My family will bear the shame of my supposed wickedness. In a hundred years from now, people will still gossip about the viscount who murdered his servant."

"Or they will praise the viscount who refused to bow to threats. You have no notion how this will all end. You do not strike me as a man who would allow such treatment. To do nothing will mean the shame of failure will eat away at you until you are withered and broken."

"And what if someone gets hurt in the process?"

"People are already hurt. How do you think your brother feels to know you have been harbouring such secrets and did not trust him enough to tell him?"

"My reasons for secrecy had nothing to do with trust."

"I understand that. Your intention is always to protect others. But perhaps they do not want your protection. Perhaps they want to stand at your side and fight with you. Either way, you must be honest. You must allow them to make their own choices."

That was what he feared most. Lucas and Helena were not the sort of people to sit back and let someone else control their destiny. Injustice was a cause close to their hearts.

Anthony sighed. He dragged his hand through his hair. "You're right. Honesty must be the way forward. I shall begin by confiding in my brother."

"To do anything else means you have surrendered to your enemies. And I know you could not live with that."

The gentle breeze picked up tempo, whipped tendrils of golden hair about her face. She was his angel of light in so many ways. Her words had the power of clarity. Her lips had the power to heal.

He brushed the curls from her face, took the edges of her cloak and pulled them together. "And what about you, Miss Roxbury? Will you teach a foolish man a lesson? Will you take me to task for my earlier comments and leave for Hagley Manor?"

She chuckled. "So now you are giving me a choice."

"I am."

"Then I choose to help you. I choose to remain by your side on this wild and reckless journey. I choose to trust that all will be well."

A wave of euphoria swept over him. It gave him confidence in his ability to succeed, and the strength he needed to talk to Lucas.

"I count myself the most privileged of men," he began, almost choking on a sudden surge of emotion. "Your beauty radiates from you like the light from the brightest star. I have noticed the way other men look at you though they are only able to glimpse your true magnificence. Your strength, your integrity, your determination to do what is right is utterly mesmerising. Indeed, I am captivated. I find I can do nothing but stand in awe."

Her hand fluttered to her heart, and she sucked in a deep breath. "That's the nicest thing anyone has ever said to me." Her gaze fell to his lips. "You say you can do nothing, but I am sure you'll think of a way to express your appreciation before we return to the house."

Good lord, the lady certainly knew how to tempt a man.

She stood before him cast in a silvery moonlit shimmer. Her lips were a deep pink, slightly swollen from their earlier encounter. There was something sensual and sinfully wicked about the inviting look in her blue eyes. Knowing there was nothing but a single layer of material covering her curvaceous body caused a lustful stirring in his loins.

"It is not often words fail me. But in this instance, I find I am rather thankful for it."

She raised a curious brow. "You are? And why is that?"

"For now, there is only one way to worship you as you deserve," he whispered as his lips met hers.

CHAPTER 12

a grey morning mist shrouded the old stone cottage like a widow's veil. The rain pelted the gravel path, lashing out at anything that stood in its way. The pebble-sized drops hammered the windows, whipped at Anthony's boots as he stood and stared at the wooden door.

"What the hell are we waiting for?" Lucas brushed the sleeves of his coat, flicked the excess droplets from his fingers as he sheltered under the porch canopy. "Please tell me you have the key."

Anthony reached into the pocket of his waistcoat and removed the small iron object. "I need a moment. It's been months since I entered the cottage."

Lucas sighed. "Then allow me to assist you." His tone conveyed an element of sympathy as he took the key. "I expect every time you enter you imagine seeing the same grisly scene."

Anthony focused on the paint-chipped door. "I shall never forget it. One would think the images would become hazy over time, that certain aspects would be forgotten. It is not so."

Lucas turned the key, had to push at the swollen wood to gain entrance. They stepped over the threshold, paused in the narrow hallway.

"You should have spoken to me," Lucas reiterated for the hundredth time. "I could have helped you." He raised his hand as Anthony opened his mouth to put forward his defence. "I understand your reasons. Let us not speak of it again."

"You're hurt, and I'm sorry. But I cannot change what I've done. What matters is that you are here with me now."

Lucas narrowed his gaze. "I trust you have told me everything."

Anthony's heart hammered against his ribs. He straightened in preparation. The next few minutes would be hard to bear.

"Almost everything."

"Almost everything? Bloody hell! What more can there be?"

Anthony had spent two hours alone with Lucas in his study recapping the events, much to Helena's chagrin. He had listened to his brother's vitriolic curses upon learning about the letters and the walking cane, watched him stomp about the room as though ready to throttle the first man who dared to question his right to be angry.

The worst was yet to come.

"As I told you earlier," Anthony began, "on the first day of every month I receive a letter, reminding me of all I have to lose should I pursue the matter of Emily's death. Along with a black feather, the missive also includes a demand for … for five hundred pounds. It is the price of silence."

Lucas gasped. "Five hundred pounds?" He shook his head and took a step back. "Five hundred pounds! Are you telling me the bastard has tried to blackmail you?"

Anthony looked to the floor. He could not bear to see disappointment in his brother's eyes. He could not bear to be reminded of his inadequacy.

"For the love of God, Anthony, please tell me you did not pay."

Shame gave way to anger. "What was I supposed to do? I could not risk a scandal. I needed time to formulate a plan. Should the evidence be presented, no jury in the land would acquit me."

Lucas dragged his hand down his face. "Heavens above. You paid the bastard five hundred pounds?"

If only that had been the end of the matter. But like all those of a rapacious disposition, no matter how much they have, they always want more.

"No." Anthony cleared his throat. "Over the months it has amounted to … to two thousand."

Lucas gulped. His eyes bulged. "God damn it." He turned on his heels and punched the air, hugged his head with arms as though protecting himself from an expected blow. "And I thought you were supposed to be the sensible one." He swung around, the muscles in his jaw hard, rigid. "That is it. I want the names of the men who stayed here, and I want them now." He stabbed his finger at the floor with such vehemence one could imagine it a deadly weapon.

"What, you think beating them all to a pulp will provide a solution?" Anthony said, though his hands throbbed just thinking of the immense feeling of satisfaction it would bring. "Hell, if it were that easy, I would break every knuckle to accomplish the task."

"Please tell me your revelation is the jaw-dropping denouement of this particular drama. Or is there more you've failed to mention? Have you signed your estate over to a charity for orphans? Or perhaps you have chosen your beloved horse to be your beneficiary."

"You have no right to mock. When people accused you of killing Lord Banbury, did you strive to clear your name? Did you beat everyone to within an inch of their life in the hope of discovering the truth?"

"It is not the same. I went to Boston believing I had killed a man. I punched him. He died. You have done nothing to warrant any of this, yet you have willingly bowed down to his extortionate demands."

"You think I have done nothing?" Anthony sneered. "You have no idea what I've been through these last few months."

"No. How would I know? You did not trust me enough to tell me."

There it was again: another opportunity to drive his point home. Anthony was a fool to think Lucas would forget his misdemeanour. His brother was a man of strong passions. He acted first, thought later. Loyalty meant everything to him. He was stubborn. Unforgiving.

"This is not going to work." Anthony stepped back. "I feel like a man staring at the hangman's noose knowing there is no hope of reprieve. I was already in the process of formulating a plan to deal with the problem, but I will do so alone."

"The hell you will." Lucas closed the gap between them and grabbed Anthony's arm. "We are in this together, whether you like it or—"

Lucas stopped abruptly. He stared at a point beyond Anthony's shoulder. The door to Emily's bedchamber was ajar. It was the reason Anthony faced the parlour. Indeed, the hairs on his nape prickled to attention at the thought of the gruesome sight lurking in the shadows behind.

Without uttering another word, Lucas pushed past him.

The door creaked open, the sound reminiscent of a tortured groan, begging for someone to put an end to its misery.

"Good Lord. No wonder you cannot get the image from your mind. Now I understand why you refused to let Helena and Miss Roxbury accompany us."

Anthony took a moment to compose himself before turning round. "I've not touched a thing since that night. Should a case ever be brought against me, I hoped there would be something here to prove my innocence."

He followed Lucas into the room. They came to a stop near the foot of the bed.

A heavy silence filled the air.

Only a few faint smears of blood tainted the white sheet. There were large claret stains on the pillows, red misshapen splatters sprayed over the wall behind the bed.

"He used the coverlet to wrap the body, hence the lack of blood on the sheets." Anthony pointed to the dusty wooden floor. "Drops of blood led to the front door, though they are hardly noticeable now."

Anthony followed Lucas' gaze to the smashed pottery on the side table, to the broken glass in the picture frame. A chair was upturned. Torn undergarments littered the floor. Two crystal glasses stood on the overmantel, the last drop of port in the bottom now a burgundy powdery residue.

"It is obvious there was a struggle." Lucas gestured to the crib near the fireplace. "Is that where you found the child?"

"Yes. There was not a speck of blood on him. But his nightclothes were sodden."

"Then that accounts for one of the odd smells lingering in here." Lucas wandered about the room. "What reason did you have for visiting? After all, you employed Emily Compton as a servant in the house."

"I received a note from her asking me to call."

"Did she say why?"

"Just that she had a problem and needed help. I was aware she was involved in a liaison with a guest but did not know who."

"Was the front door open when you arrived?"

Anthony shook his head. "I could hear William crying. When Emily failed to answer, I went back to the house to get the key."

Lucas sighed. "Then whoever killed her must have still been in the house. When you returned, did you notice anything untoward?" He waved his hand in the air. "Other than a dead body I mean."

Anthony closed his eyes for a moment and pictured the scene. "All the curtains were closed though it was not yet dusk."

"So you found Emily in bed when you returned?"

Anthony blinked several times. "I assumed she was asleep. I called out to her but received no response. The room was cold, the fire nothing but glowing embers in the grate. William would not stop crying. It was not until I lit the candle that the true horror of what had occurred became apparent."

"You're certain she was dead?"

"If you had seen her eyes, seen the blood dripping from a wound on her head, the crimson pool on the coverlet, then you would not ask me such a question."

Lucas gave an apologetic shrug. "It is worth considering the point that she may have wrapped the coverlet around her shoulders and staggered from here looking for help."

"I have searched every foot of ground from here to Witham. I have scoured the woods, beaten at the undergrowth in the hope she may have done what you suggest." Indeed, he had not slept for the first few nights. "I spent two weeks outdoors. But then I received the first letter confirming she was dead."

"You have his confession on paper?"

"Of course not. He spoke as a witness, spoke only of my guilt. But he knew too much. He described the scene, taunted me with the feather. In a weird way, one has to admire the way he executes a plan. He certainly has the wherewithal to make me look a fool."

Lucas walked over to stand in front of him. "You're no fool, Anthony. Your mind is consumed with trying to do what is right for others. You've not stopped to think of yourself. You want an end to this nightmare. You want Miss Roxbury in every way a man could want a woman. And I am going to help you achieve your task." Lucas patted him on the upper arm. "Well, only the first task. I am sure you are more than capable of managing the second one on your own."

"And will I be forced to listen to your constant complaints about my misgivings?"

"Without a doubt. I am like a dog with a bone when I have a point to make. But you need me. I am hotheaded and seek to use my fists to deal with my problems. You are even tempered and seek a logical answer to your woes. Together we make for a much more formidable opponent."

"And what if Fate works against us?"

"Then we go down fighting. We go down together." Lucas winked. "But I can assure you that won't happen."

A smile threatened to form on Anthony's lips. His brother's confidence was contagious. "Do you have a plan?"

"Of course. But we must return to town as a matter of urgency."

"Town?" The thought caused a sudden ache in his chest. It would mean sending Miss Roxbury to Hagley Manor.

"We can achieve nothing rusticating in the country. On

our return, our first objective will be to locate Mr Thorpe. Without him, Mr Weston never would have confessed. Without him, we would not have discovered the truth about Lord Banbury. Indeed, I find it odd that you have not thought of contacting him yourself."

For all that was holy. He was not a complete imbecile.

"I told you, I have not been sitting about idle. As soon as I received the blackmail note, I made the necessary enquiries in the hope Mr Thorpe would take my case. It appears he has retired. Ill health prevents him from pursuing his previous line of work."

"Ill health? I know he wore a white wig, but my guess is he isn't a day over thirty. What of Mr Bostock? Perhaps he might be able to persuade his master to see us."

"Bostock? We have no hope of finding him."

Lucas cast an arrogant grin. "That is why you need my help. A man of Bostock's size and brawn doesn't wile away his days in the circulating library. He will need an outlet for all that pent-up rage, somewhere to go to maintain his physical prowess."

"And you know of such a place?" Anthony mocked.

"I think you forget I spent four years with a bare-knuckle fighter from Cork. Indeed, had we more time I would have sent for O'Brien. Men like that are hungry for a scuffle. They have too much energy racing through their veins."

For the first time in months, hope blossomed in Anthony's chest. Until now, trying to imagine the future was like trying to see the bottom of a murky pond. No matter how hard he focused, all still looked bleak.

"You are yet to realise the importance of the date," Anthony said.

Lucas looked at him blankly.

"I am to make another deposit of five hundred pounds, four days hence."

"Four days?" Lucas scratched his head. "That does not give us much time. How do you make this deposit? Surely not with the bank."

"I am given a time and place. The locations are always different. I am told to leave the notes in a leather satchel, warned that should I try to intervene then the world will learn of my penchant for murder."

Lucas narrowed his gaze. "I assume you've waited to see who comes to collect the bag?"

Anthony nodded. "It's never the same person. I've attempted to follow them, but the money changes hands at least two or three times. They use the back streets and alleys. I am forced to follow on foot, and they always have a hackney waiting to transport them to God only knows where. I don't know the streets well enough to anticipate their movements."

"All the more reason we need the help of Bostock and Thorpe," Lucas said. "They strike me as men who have spent enough time on the streets to know their way about."

"Then I pray you have more luck finding them than I did."

Lucas scanned the room. "We should conduct another search before we leave for London. Perhaps we might stumble upon a clue."

"I doubt it. During those first few weeks, I scoured every room. More times than I care to mention. Emily was determined to keep the identity of her suitor a secret."

Lucas exhaled deeply. "Then let us go back to the house and inform the ladies of our impending departure. I imagine the news will not be well received. Helena is determined to help you, despite the delicate nature of her con—" He paused. "Did you hear that?"

Anthony strained to listen. "It sounds like someone whistling. It is probably the gardener going about his duties."

Lucas frowned. "Then why do I have an odd feeling in the pit of my stomach?" Without uttering another word, he strode from the room.

Anthony followed his brother outside, noted a stationary carriage on the lane nearby. "Those horses look like your new matching pair. Is that not your coachman?"

"What the blazes is he doing here?"

Panic flared in Anthony's chest when he considered the possibility of Miss Roxbury leaving without saying goodbye. There was so much he wanted to say. But perhaps now was not the time to make promises he might not be able to keep.

"Helena must have instructed him to take Miss Roxbury home."

They did not have an opportunity to contemplate the event further.

Helena stuck her head out of the carriage window. "Lucas. Lucas." She waved at them and, upon securing her husband's attention, blew him a kiss. "Don't be angry," she shouted. "I am escorting Miss Roxbury to London. I love you."

They watched with open mouths as she closed the window and the carriage rattled off along the lane. A minute passed before either of them spoke.

Anthony rubbed his chin. "Well, I was going to suggest that Miss Roxbury return to Hagley Manor whilst we conduct our investigation."

"I believe my wife anticipated your move and has other ideas. When we reach London, remind me to give Jackson a lecture on being loyal to his master."

"You do not seem overly concerned about the fact."

Lucas chuckled. "Don't mistake me. I fear for Miss Roxbury's reputation. But I have cause to celebrate."

"How so?" Anthony said, somewhat bemused, although he could not deny his body thrummed with excitement at the thought of seeing Miss Roxbury again so soon.

"Knowing of your obsession with honour, Helena will ensure you've no choice but to marry Sarah Roxbury. Judging by the way you salivate excessively when you look at her, I suspect my wife knows what she is doing."

Anthony cast Lucas a sidelong glance. "You seem rather happy at the prospect."

"Oh, I am pleased for you. But it is for selfish reasons I find my mood much improved. Helena will feel she has to make amends for her irresponsible behaviour and I cannot help but relish the anticipation of what our reunion will bring."

"Well, whatever happens during the next few days, I doubt our lives will be the same." Anthony should have been thinking about Emily Compton, about catching a murderer before losing another five hundred pounds. But a vision of a golden-haired beauty filled his head. The prospect of kissing her soft lips was an incentive to hurry and be on their way. "Come. Let us go and rouse Carter and see if his driving skills are a match for your coachman. We cannot be outdone by ladies."

"Let them think they've won." Lucas patted Anthony on the back. "Come nightfall, Miss Roxbury will be begging to be back in your favour."

CHAPTER 13

*M*uffled masculine voices rumbled through the hall. Sarah strained to listen for evidence of their gruff, disgruntled intonation. She glanced up at the clock on the mantel in the drawing room. They had arrived at the Dempseys' townhouse two hours ago and knew Lord Harwood and Mr Dempsey would not be far behind.

"Do you think they will be terribly angry?" Sarah said, though judging by the smug look on Helena's face, she did not need to worry.

Helena shuffled to the edge of her seat. "They will pretend to be annoyed. No doubt we will have a lecture on the dangers two ladies face when travelling alone on our treacherous roads."

"What will they say when you tell them that, whilst they conversed in the study, we broke into the cottage and conducted our own investigation?"

It took two hairpins and a little patience for Helena to click the lever and open the back door. A man by the name of O'Brien had taught her the art should she ever find herself in a predicament.

Amusement flashed in Helena's eyes. "We won't tell them that part just yet. But when they broach the subject of the cottage, I must tell them the truth. Indeed, I am intrigued to see if they reached the same conclusions we did."

The thirty minutes spent in Emily Compton's home had been the most harrowing of Sarah's life. It was not the sight of splattered blood she found disturbing. It was not the pungent smell that permeated the air, or the eerie chill that penetrated her bones.

It was the crude wooden crib standing empty and abandoned in the corner.

Her heart ached at the thought of the helpless babe she had cradled in her arms. Her soul yearned to ease the suffering of the man left to shoulder the responsibility alone.

"Now, remember what I said." Helena kept her voice low as she focused her attention on the door handle. "We must discover the names of the gentlemen who attended the house party if we are to meet with Mrs Chambers later this evening. We will tell Anthony and Lucas everything once she has agreed to take the case."

Sarah had to admit there was something intriguing about a female enquiry agent. What was Mrs Chambers' story? How was she equipped to deal with the criminal fraternity?

"And what if the gentlemen remain at home tonight?" Sarah asked, knowing she would feel disappointed if they were unable to meet with this mysterious woman.

"They won't," Helena said with an air of confidence. "As soon as I saw the dreadful scene in the cottage, I knew there was little point remaining at Elton Park. Lucas will be itching to discover all he can about the gentlemen who attended the party. He will wish to rule them out one by one until left with the scoundrel responsible."

Sarah sensed a hint of trepidation in Helena's voice. "And

what will Mr Dempsey do when he discovers the name of the man responsible?"

Helena's expression darkened. "He would give his life to save his brother, to save me from the shame of disgrace." For the first time since meeting Helena, Sarah noted a flicker of fear in her usually warm eyes. With a sudden shake of the head it was gone. "Which is why we must try to help them if we can."

"There is every chance your maid will return with bad news. I suspect a woman of Mrs Chambers' notoriety will not be sitting indoors with her sewing whilst waiting for her next client."

"If she cannot see us this evening, then—" Helena stopped abruptly.

The gentlemen entered the drawing room. While their rigid jaws and thin mouths conveyed disapproval, a hint of amusement flashed in their eyes.

Helena jumped to her feet and waited for her husband to approach. "Are you terribly angry with me?" She placed her hand on his chest. "Your heart is racing. Perhaps you are in dire need of refreshment after such a tiresome journey."

A smile touched the corners of Mr Dempsey's mouth. "I believe that is exactly what I need. I wish to speak to you alone. Perhaps we could step outside."

"Of course. Shall we go to the parlour?"

"That should suffice." Mr Dempsey inclined his head to his brother. "Excuse us for a moment."

Sarah's pulse raced when Anthony Dempsey turned to face her. He waited until the door clicked shut before closing the gap between them. "Miss Roxbury. It's a pleasure to see you again so soon." He inclined his head yet his sparkling blue eyes held her gaze.

The air about them thrummed with the same nervous,

excitable energy she found so utterly addictive. Sarah swallowed deeply. She had not seen him since the previous evening. When he had escorted her from the garden and kissed her beneath a blanket of a thousand stars.

"My lord." She offered a curtsy, despite struggling to stop her legs from trembling. "I trust you are not too displeased to find that your houseguest upped and left without a word of thanks or gratitude."

"I think *concerned* would be the most accurate definition. I find nothing displeasing about anything you do, Miss Roxbury."

Desire pulsed in her core. Oh, how she longed to hear her given name breeze from his lips once again. How she longed to appease this strange clawing need. Indeed, it took her a moment to catch her breath. "It's kind of you to say so. But I am sure you are burning to know why we left Elton Park so abruptly."

He glanced briefly at the door before leaning forward. "An intense burning is definitely the sensation I feel flowing through my veins at this precise moment." He spoke slowly yet with purpose. "And you are right. My need is urgent. My desire for fulfilment is bordering on desperation."

The seductive power of his voice washed over her in warm waves.

"Then your need must be contagious," she replied brazenly. "For now I feel it, too."

He inhaled deeply, devoured her with his heated stare. "You do know the danger you face in coming back to town?"

She shrugged. "The man responsible for Emily's death has more things to worry about than frightening me with his silly feathers."

"I was referring to the fact we will be spending more time

in each other's company." He moistened his lips, and she found she could not tear her gaze away from his mouth. "I have recently discovered you are the only person with the ability to weaken my rigid stance, to melt my usual steely reserve."

Fire flared in her chest, flowed down to the apex of her thighs to throb and pulse. The intense heat inside made it difficult to breathe. His words gave her the confidence to be bold.

"Then we should put your theory to the test." She placed her hand on his cheek. "No. You have not melted yet, my lord." She ran her hand slowly over his chest, trailed her finger down over the buttons on his waistcoat. "How do you feel now? Do you feel your control slipping?"

"I think you know the answer."

In a move both swift and sudden, he pulled her close and covered her mouth to ravage her senseless. He tasted divine. His potent scent fed her craving. Overcome with an uncontrollable feeling of longing, she was the one who penetrated his mouth with her tongue. His hum of approval caused a pleasurable throb between her thighs. Large, powerful hands caressed her buttocks through her gown.

She could not get enough of him. Every fibre of her being needed more. Every part of her body needed to feel his touch.

A groan resonated from the back of his throat and she knew then, as she teetered on the brink of something utterly magical, that she would willingly take him into her eager body.

Perhaps it was the shock of how much she wanted him that forced her from her idyllic playground. With her senses a little more in tune with her surroundings she heard the Dempseys' loud chatter beyond the door.

"Your ... your brother" was all she managed to say as she stepped out of Anthony's grasp. Good lord. She put her hand to her chest. The erratic beat of her heart vibrated against her palm.

The look on Anthony's face spoke of satisfaction, of supreme confidence in his ability to please. They were still standing in the middle of the room, hungry, desperate, unable to look at anything else but each other.

The door handle rattled, loud voices permeated the tense silence as Helena and Lucas Dempsey returned.

"Cook is preparing a light repast after our long journey," Mr Dempsey said as he threw himself into the chair. "There is no need to stand. There are other chairs. You do not have to wait for us to invite you to sit, Miss Roxbury."

Helena's giggle forced Sarah to blink a few times. She cleared her throat in an attempt to bring her thoughts back to the present.

"After you, Miss Roxbury," Anthony said as he gestured to the blue damask sofa.

Sarah's legs practically buckled. She flopped into the seat. Her body trembled with an irrepressible energy, whilst her mind was lost in a mass of fluffy clouds.

Anthony sat down beside her. "Your face is flushed," he whispered. His fingers brushed against her hand resting on the pad of the seat, a discreet touch that held a wealth of promise. "It is rather becoming."

She pressed the back of her fingers to her cheeks. No doubt her whole body was as red as a berry.

A footman entered carrying a tea tray. He placed it on the low table in front of them and while Helena took over the task of pouring, the distraction gave Sarah an opportunity to reply to Anthony's comment.

"I … I concede to your better judgement," Sarah said discreetly as her heart slowed to a normal pace. "It appears your assessment was correct."

"How so?" A smile touched his lips. The sight always made her giddy.

"If we continue in the same manner, we are both in danger of losing our heads."

"If we continue in the same manner, I fear you are in danger of losing a lot more," he replied.

It took a second or two for her to comprehend his meaning. Then, she could not shake the image of his naked torso from her mind. She touched her face again. Heavens. Her cheeks were hot enough to keep a small family warm on a bitter winter's morning.

"I took the liberty of informing Helena of our plans this evening." Mr Dempsey directed his attention to his brother. "She assures me they have no desire to accompany us."

Anthony turned to her. "We are to go out in the hope of locating Mr Thorpe. He is the gentleman who helped prove Lucas' innocence in the death of Lord Banbury."

"As you are aware, it is not safe to wander the streets at night." Mr Dempsey spoke with an element of caution. "It would only hinder our investigation should you insist on coming, too."

"We have no desire to go traipsing through the back streets of London in search of your enquiry agent," Helena said. Well, it was not a lie. "Do we, Miss Roxbury?"

Sarah shook her head. "No. But you must tell us the names of the gentlemen under suspicion. If this Mr Thorpe fellow is to conduct an investigation, I feel it is vital you reveal all you know."

"I am not sure I agree." Anthony sat back and folded his

arms across his chest. "The temptation to approach them would prove too great." He was referring to Helena's inquisitive nature, of course.

"So you are saying you do not trust us with the information?" Helena countered.

"No. I did not say that."

Sarah turned to face Anthony. "You are not thinking logically." From his shocked expression, coupled with Helena's discreet gasp, the gentleman was not used to being challenged on his mental prowess. "The man responsible for Emily's death is watching you. Else why would he have thrust the feather into my palm at Lord Daleforth's ball? In this case, ignorance is not bliss. I could accept an invitation to ride in the park, never knowing that the gentleman at my side is responsible for a whole host of horrendous crimes."

"Miss Roxbury is right," Helena said.

"I, too, am inclined to agree," Mr Dempsey added.

Anthony narrowed his gaze as he rubbed his chin. "You would accept an invitation to ride in the park?"

The question caught her unawares. He seemed more perturbed by the thought she would welcome another man's attention than be duped by a cold-blooded killer.

"The comment was made purely to convey my point." She paused. Whilst she was not in the habit of playing coquette, Anthony Dempsey needed to know she would not wait for him forever. "Even so, I received many offers to ride out when last in town."

His blue eyes turned a hard, steely grey. "Then I must politely ask you to decline should another offer be made."

Pursing her lips was the only way to stop a smile from forming. "Is that because you fear for my safety?"

"Of course."

"Then you should divulge the names of your suspects, for

I find I am sometimes far too polite to say no. It is a weakness of mine."

"I shall hold that thought for future reference." The amused look in Anthony's eyes faded. "You must assure me you have no intention of approaching any of the men."

Sarah looked deep into his eyes. "You have my word I will not approach any of the men named without your prior knowledge."

Anthony inclined his head. "Helena? I will hear your assurance, too."

Helena sighed. "I have no desire to confront a man who may be guilty of murdering an innocent woman."

"Very well," he said begrudgingly. "The gentlemen who attended the party at Elton Park were Lord Nettleson, Lord Faversham and Mr James St. John." He paused. "Mr Robert Fraser arrived late, accompanied by … by Lord Barton."

"Barton?" Helena blurted. "But he danced with Miss Roxbury at Lord Daleforth's ball."

An ice-cold chill crept over Sarah's shoulders, forcing her to shudder. Was the Earl of Barton's affable manner merely a mode of deception? Of course, it was not only Lord Barton's motives that roused her suspicion.

"Is that why you lied about having a place on my dance card?" Numb and wracked with disappointment, she longed to hear his answer. What a fool she was to assume his arrogant countenance stemmed from jealousy.

"My primary objective has always been to protect you." His evasive reply, whilst satisfying on one level, left her questioning his true feelings.

"Now is not the time to press you further," she said, "but we will discuss the matter upon your return this evening."

He inclined his head.

"So, where will you begin your search for the elusive Mr Thorpe?" Helena said.

Anthony sat forward. "There is a man employed at White's who makes it his business to assist gentlemen with their needs. Whatever they may be. You would be surprised at the depth of his knowledge. Indeed, there is not an event in London that he does not know of. He is the man who first informed me of Mr Thorpe's skill as an enquiry agent."

Surely they were not pinning all their hopes on finding one man.

"And what if you cannot locate him?" Sarah shuffled uncomfortably. She prayed Mrs Chambers would prove to be available. "What if he refuses to offer his assistance? Is there nothing else we can do in the meantime?"

A morbid silence ensued.

"You could always book me on the next ship to Boston," Anthony said. "I believe that is where one goes when accused of a murder they did not commit."

Sarah stood next to Helena on the pavement in New Bond Street and stared up at the dimly lit building. While other modistes packed their windows with examples of their lavish gowns, Madame Fontaine chose a subtle approach.

A curtain of diaphanous material prevented the onlooker from examining the dress on display. You could see it was a dark shade of red. You could notice the sparkle of jewels on the bodice. The matching silk slippers were placed in full view on a gold velvet stool with excessive fringing. In its entirety, the scene created an air of mystery, of elegant sophistication.

Sarah threaded her arm through Helena's and stepped

closer to the bow window. "I must say, it is a testament to Mrs Chambers' professionalism as an enquiry agent that she should arrange to meet us in such a convenient place."

"Not only that," Helena said with the same hint of admiration, "but Madame Fontaine is a highly skilled modiste. Appointments require more than a month's notice. That she should allow Mrs Chambers use of her shop shows the lady is well respected."

A frisson of excitement coursed through Sarah's veins. While she had once been content to sit at home with her sewing, she found the idea of secret liaisons much more thrilling.

Of course, it helped that Helena conveyed nothing but a determination to succeed in their mission. Indeed, Helena's confidence was infectious.

"Did your maid say what we are supposed to do?"

Helena glanced back over her shoulder. "We are to knock on the front door. Apparently, she often gives her clients evening appointments."

"It is all rather mysterious. Meetings arranged via a back room in a coffee house. Clandestine consultations in a modiste's shop. Whatever should we expect next?"

Helena shrugged. "I think Mrs Chambers is too unpredictable to say. It was Lord Banbury who first mentioned her to me. Perhaps he thought that in marrying Lucas I might find myself embroiled in scandal. Indeed, his ex-mistress was somewhat of a gossip, though I hear she has since escaped her creditors and run away to Italy with Lord Lindford."

It was a credit to the strength of the Dempseys' marriage that Helena could speak so openly about a subject most women would refuse to acknowledge.

"Does … does Lord Harwood have a mistress?" Sarah felt

a sharp pang in her chest at the thought of him with any other woman.

Helena's eyes grew wide. "Anthony is not the sort of gentleman to take a mistress. Oh, I don't doubt he has had numerous discreet liaisons. But they will have been with respectable widows, intelligent companions as opposed to lustful leeches."

Sarah chuckled at Helena's amusing comment for it deflected all jealous thoughts from taking root and festering. "I don't suppose it's a secret that I've developed a deep attachment to him."

It was Helena's turn to laugh. "Nor is it a secret he is totally enamoured with you. His insistence on always doing the right thing means he can often appear cold and aloof. But I have never seen him look at a woman the way he looks at you."

After their heated exchange in the drawing room, *cold* was not a word Sarah would use to describe Anthony Dempsey. Beneath his reserve, she found him to be wildly passionate, utterly irresistible.

"I hope he will not be too angry that we have employed Mrs Chambers to investigate the gentlemen who attended the party."

"You do understand why I must tell them where we have been? I cannot lie to Lucas. It is bad enough I have withheld information, but I know of no other way to help them."

The sudden tinkling of a bell made Sarah jump.

"Do you intend to come in or are you happy to gape at the window for the entire evening?" The authoritative voice carried a mild hint of humour.

They turned their attention to the woman standing in the doorway. The curvaceous silhouette revealed a person with perfect posture. Indeed, there was something stately, something regal about her demeanour.

Sarah cleared her throat. "Madame Fontaine?"

"I'm afraid she is otherwise engaged."

Helena stepped forward. "We are here to see Mrs Chambers."

"I see. Then you had better come inside."

CHAPTER 14

*T*he fracas on the steps of White's involved a podgy gentleman whose request for membership had been blackballed, and who now refused to move unless the clubmen held another ballot.

Ignoring the furore, Anthony pushed past the flustered footmen, eager to reach his conveyance waiting on the opposite side of St. James' Street.

"We need to go to Marylebone," Anthony informed his coachman. He flipped open his gold pocket watch beneath the light of the carriage lamp, checked the time and snapped it shut. "The house is in Russell Place, but you are to drive into the mews off London Street."

Carter nodded and tipped his hat. "Aye, my lord."

Anthony climbed inside the vehicle and dropped into the seat opposite Lucas. "You should have come into the club for a drink. You could have downed a brandy while I spoke to Horbury."

Lucas folded his arms across his chest and sneered. "I would rather gouge my eyes with the sharp nib of a quill pen than spend a minute in that place."

"It is an elite club," Anthony said, finding his brother's disdain amusing. "Our father and grandfather were members. Could you not forsake your pride in an effort to maintain tradition?"

"Tradition!" Lucas scoffed. "If you are looking for someone to follow in our ancestors' footsteps, then you had better produce an heir. Should I inherit I shall tell them in no uncertain terms what they can do with their membership."

"Where would you go when in need of male company for the evening?" Anthony enjoyed teasing him. If nothing else, it passed the time.

"Why would I seek male companionship when I have everything I need at home? Besides, when in town, I can call on you. I have no desire to spend time with men who wear their coats inside out to bring them luck at the tables. Nor am I inclined to gossip like a fishwife or gamble my inheritance on a single game of whist."

"I thought Helena had driven the cynic out of you."

Lucas raised an arrogant brow. "I think you'll find Helena likes me just as I am."

There was a truth to his words that roused a sliver of envy. "Then you are amongst the luckiest of men. Love and acceptance are things we all aspire to experience."

"If love and acceptance are what you seek, then it seems you have found them. Miss Roxbury is in love with you." Lucas paused. "She readily accepted your word on this whole debacle. She has put her reputation at risk to give you her support."

Was Sarah Roxbury in love with him?

During times of wistful fancy, he imagined it was true. But his mind had been a jumbled mess of contradictions of late, to the point he could no longer trust his own thoughts.

"Miss Roxbury is not in love with me. Though I cannot

deny we share an indefinable attraction." More than an attraction. The feelings ran deep, were utterly profound. She was the last thing he thought about after climbing into bed at night. She monopolised his waking thoughts, too. "But perhaps you are confusing compassion and kindness for something more."

Lucas opened his mouth to speak but then stopped and shook his head. "No doubt you are right. There's no denying she is beautiful, but that has never been enough for you. I suspect you would be ill-suited when it came to conversing intelligently."

A fire ignited in Anthony's chest: an urgent need to defend and protect. "Then you do not know her as I do. Miss Roxbury is the most interesting, most intelligent, most captivating woman I've ever met. I fear I am the one who falls short of her expectations in every regard."

A mischievous smile played on Lucas' lips. "I did not realise you felt so passionately about her. If you want her, you'd better do your damnedest to let her know how you feel."

Anthony released a long, weary sigh. "When this is all over I intend to do just that."

"Excellent. I shall cling to the hope that I will not be left to care for you in your old age."

"With your reckless temperament, there is every chance I shall outlive *you*." The comment failed to amuse. Fear crept upon Anthony suddenly. Whatever happened during the next few days, it was his responsibility to ensure Lucas kept his head. "Just promise me you will think before you act."

Lucas stretched his arms and yawned. "You have enough to contend with. Stop worrying about me." He glanced out of the window, at the street shrouded in blanket of fog. "As you have not mentioned where we are heading, I assume

Horbury offered some insight into where you might locate Thorpe."

"Horbury makes it his business to know everything about everyone." Anthony had paid three pounds for the pleasure. "It is how he makes a living. But Horbury reiterated that the enquiry agent he first told me of has since retired."

Lucas sighed. "So what are we to do now?"

"Horbury informed me of a sporting event, held every Thursday and Friday evening at a house in Russell Place. He said the agent who assisted us two years ago might be found there. Apparently, boxing is a more lucrative venture than solving the problems of Society's preened prigs."

Lucas jerked his head back. "Horbury called you a preened prig? I trust you did not leave the man standing."

"He was not referring to me, but merely speaking in general."

"Well, whether we find Thorpe or not," Lucas began as he settled back in his seat, "the night will not be a complete waste of time. It's been an age since I watched a good fight. I've yet to witness a man with O'Brien's strength and agility."

"You'll not have time to watch anything. Horbury intimated we would struggle to identify Thorpe from our previous association with him. Our task will be to observe the crowd in the hope of locating him."

"Then the night will most certainly prove interesting, in more ways than one."

To anyone passing through Russell Place, number eight was just another nondescript townhouse in the middle of an equally nondescript row. The fog rendered the scene a monochrome canvas. Grey. Dull. Uninspiring. Not a single soul trudged the pavements. It was hardly the venue for sports enthusiasts eager for a night of merriment. Indeed, from the subdued appearance of the house, one would imagine they had made a mistake until they entered the cobbled stable yard located via an alley off London Street.

Huddled in small groups around glowing braziers, gentlemen scrawled in books with stubby pencils beneath their lantern lights. They ripped the leaves from their bindings and passed them to runners who raced through the mews as though the seats of their breeches were on fire, before entering the garden via a wooden gate in the stone wall.

The carriage rattled to an abrupt halt. Carter exchanged angry words with a scrawny man who had all the brawn and breadth of a tallow candle, and who proceeded to stab his finger at the entrance to the mews.

"Perhaps the event is invitation only," Lucas surmised as they watched the scene with interest. "I hope you have something with which to barter."

"You have a passion for pugilism," Anthony said with a grin. "Perhaps I should offer you up as a contender."

"While I am competent with my fists, these bouts can be savage. I'm rather partial to both of my ears and have grown used to my perfect aristocratic nose."

Carter climbed down from his perch, rapped on the window and informed them that all carriages and conveyances must be parked two streets away. No exceptions.

The soles of their shoes had barely touched the slippery stones, when a boy, no older than twelve, hurried to greet them.

"Aye, governor. Will you be wanting to place a bet?"

"Is it to be a single bout?" Lucas enquired.

"One bout, seven contenders." The boy pushed his fingers

beneath his cap and scratched his head. "The odds favour Brutus the Beast."

Who the devil called themselves Brutus the Beast? The name was obviously used to intimidate.

"Seven contenders?" Lucas pursed his lips. "Is it a case of last man standing?"

The boy nodded. "Anyone off the platform is out. All's fair but no punching below the belt. And no mufflers."

"Mufflers?" Anthony asked.

"The lad means no gloves. They are to fight with bare fists. This is not a sparring match between privileged lords at Jackson's saloon." Lucas turned to the boy. "What are the odds another man will beat this Brutus fellow?"

The boy glanced briefly back over his shoulder. "They say only The Piper stands any chance."

"The Piper." Lucas chuckled. "The name hardly rouses confidence."

"The Piper's from the Highlands. He got his name 'cause his chest's so large they say it's full of air."

Lucas reached into the pocket of his coat and removed a few gold coins. "Then I'll wager three sovereigns Brutus will lose."

"To The Piper, or to any contender?"

Lucas shrugged. "To anyone."

The boy snatched the coin and bit the metal before running to a group of men and returning with a slip of paper. "Can't see you having much luck, but all winnings are to be collected ringside."

Anthony shook his head as he watched the boy move on to another punter. "With a name like Brutus, you can say goodbye to your sovereigns."

"Have a little faith," Lucas replied as they headed through the gate into the garden. "You know I always champion the less fortunate. Miracles are known to happen."

"I took Mr Thorpe to be a scholarly sort of man," Anthony said as another runner barged past them, one hand clutching his hat, the paper in the other hand flapping about in the wind. "I imagined this form of organised gambling to be above him."

Lucas tutted. "As soon as I saw his associate, Mr Bostock, I knew they were men raised on the street. There are but a few ways to gain information from unwilling parties. Thorpe didn't strike me as a man who'd spend hard-earned money on bribes. And I imagine Bostock is sufficiently able enough with his fists to make those with a strong constitution confess."

"Whatever Mr Thorpe's story," Anthony replied, "he speaks like a gentleman, acts like a gentleman and has received some sort of formal education."

Lucas nodded. "A gentleman who knows his way around the streets would be a formidable opponent indeed."

"That is what I am hoping."

They followed the line of excited bucks and drunken rakes through the servants' quarters, and up into a long drawing room stripped of all adornments. The sound of boisterous laughter rang through the room, coupled with the incessant chatter from the hordes of men crowded into the compact space.

In the centre stood an unfenced wooden platform surrounded on all sides by several rows of crude tiered seats. Men pushed and shoved like animals packed into the slaughterhouse desperate to find a free space.

"When the seats are full, they will have no choice but to gather around the platform." Lucas gestured to the two bucks engaged in an argument over the last place on the bench.

"Standing eye level with a boxer's feet is enough to strike fear in the hearts of most men."

Anthony would be damned if he'd stay long enough to see a punch thrown. "Just scour the crowd for Mr Thorpe. The sooner we speak to him, the sooner we can be on our way."

Lucas looked most disgruntled. "I can't leave without collecting my winnings."

"Do you think any of them have a hope of beating Brutus the Beast? Heavens, a shiver shoots down my spine whenever I think about those poor blighters up against such a creature."

"All men have a weakness," Lucas said as his gaze drifted over the fifty or so men sitting in the tiered seats opposite. "One only has to read Greek mythology to know that's true."

Anthony scanned the sea of black top hats. The crowd were an eclectic mix of gentlemen, raffish scoundrels, merchants and the odd unsavoury character who did not seem to fit into any worthy category.

"Damn, Thorpe could be any one of a hundred men here," Anthony complained. "Though he had white hair at our last meeting, I'm convinced he wore a wig."

"There is every chance—" Lucas stopped abruptly, his eyes growing wide. "Wait. Is that not Mr Bostock over there, standing near the platform? He is wearing a green coat two sizes too small."

Anthony cast a discreet glance at the man in question. A frisson of excitement flowed through his veins as the sight of Mr Thorpe's associate.

Bostock was a hulking figure whose neck was swallowed by the bulging muscles in his shoulders. His square jaw and protruding brow gave the impression he was permanently at odds with the world. Should he be forced to throw his hands in the air in frustration, the material stretched tightly over sinewy arms was sure to split under the strain.

"He appears somewhat flustered," Anthony remarked. "That is the second time he has mopped his brow with his handkerchief."

"Perhaps he has wagered more than he cares on the outcome of the night's battle. We should approach him before the fight gets under way and he is too preoccupied to grant us an audience."

With Mr Bostock being a man of little patience, Anthony did not hold out any hope of moving beyond a greeting. "Very well. But from what I remember he is not a man of many words."

They pushed through the crowd, winced as the first contender appeared at the double doors and the room erupted into a cacophony of hoots and jeers. The man wore black breeches, white stockings and dainty shoes so at odds with the burly figure he cut. His hair was cropped short, too short for chubby fingers to grab. Muscles rippled in his abdomen as he flexed for the crowd. He climbed the steps to the ring, bowed to the audience purely to antagonise those betting against him.

Mr Bostock was too engrossed in the flamboyant display to notice Anthony and Lucas approach.

Anthony cleared his throat. "Mr Bostock, I wonder if I could have but a moment of your time?"

Black marble eyes flicked over them briefly. Whether he remembered them or not, he gave no indication. "Not now."

Undeterred, Anthony asked, "Do you recall assisting us with a little problem we had a couple of years ago?"

"The name of the problem was Mr Weston," Lucas clarified, stepping to the side to block Bostock's view.

Mr Bostock made no reply but stared at a point beyond

their shoulder, his frown so deep his brows overhung his eyelids. "Damn it. Where the hell has he got to?"

"We can see you're busy," Anthony said. "Just tell us where we might find Mr Thorpe, and we shall leave you to your business."

The mere mention of Thorpe caught Bostock's attention. His cold hard stare bored into them. "Mr Thorpe no longer accepts clients."

"We would make it worth his while. We would double his usual fee."

Two more fighters climbed the steps leading up to the platform. The crowd booed, people stood, pointed and shook their fists. The fighters' toned physiques were as impressive as the first opponent.

"Mr Thorpe no longer works as an enquiry agent," Bostock reiterated as he craned his neck to observe the gathering group of pugilists. "You're wasting your time here."

Anthony took a step closer. "I shall not bandy words, Mr Bostock. We are desperate men." There was little point evading the seriousness of their problem. "Will you not at least give us the opportunity of asking Thorpe ourselves?"

Mr Bostock stared up into the crowd. He could have been looking at any one of a number of men. He tapped his nose. Paused. Nodded.

"Mr Thorpe is unwilling to offer his assistance."

Anthony jerked his head back. "What, without even hearing details of our case?"

"The decision is made." Bostock's face remained impassive. "Now, if you'll excuse me I have business to—" His attention shot to a young boy pushing through the crowd towards them. "Where the hell is he?" Bostock's bulky frame swamped the slight figure. "Tell me you've found him."

The boy ripped his cap off his head and held it between

both hands. "Word is The Piper's taken off with that lady friend of his. Left their lodgings this morning. Took the stage-coach to York."

"York!" Bostock bellowed though the noise was drowned out by the rowdy crowd. He bent his head. "What the bloody hell am I to do now? If I don't put a man in that ring, I've to return all wagers. I'll not be allowed to fight here again. Tell Bagley to find me someone else. Now!"

The boy clutched his cap and shook his head. "There's no … no one else."

Only a coward sent a boy to do a man's work.

Another contender bounded up onto the stage amidst a round of raucous applause, although this fellow's muscles lay hidden beneath rolls of fat. A scuffle broke out as the four men vied for the best position.

Bostock rubbed the back of his neck, the material of his coat straining under the pressure. Anthony considered his muscular frame. Surely Bostock was equipped to step into the ring.

"You look like a man capable of handling any situation," Lucas said, coming to the same conclusion. "Can you not fight in The Piper's place?"

Bostock shook his head. "If I could, I would." The sudden glint in his eye suggested he'd like nothing more than to put his fists to work. "As the trainer, it's against the damn rules." He glanced up into the mass of hats, swiped his fingers across his neck and shrugged.

Despite the din, an eerie silence filled Anthony's head. It was like a moment of calm out at sea—when one knew the approaching wave gathered momentum and would soon come crashing down to destroy the equilibrium.

"Look. I've been trained to box by the best bare-knuckle fighter in Ireland," Lucas said. His words were of tidal wave proportion. "I'm not saying I can win, but I can last a round or two."

"There are no rounds in this fight. You'll need stamina as well as strength."

"It won't be a problem."

After recovering from the initial shock, Anthony grabbed his brother's arm. "Are you insane? They'll beat you to a pulp."

"No, they won't," Lucas replied with an arrogant grin.

Bostock folded his meaty arms across his chest and narrowed his gaze. "What's his name, this fighter you know?"

"O'Brien."

"Shamus O'Brien?"

Lucas nodded. "We met on the crossing to Boston."

Bostock made a series of hand gestures to the crowd before rubbing his chubby chin. "And you'd be willing to go up against Brutus the Beast?" His beady eyes scanned Lucas' face. "You'd leave with a scar or two."

"He is not setting foot on that platform," Anthony cried. What the hell was Lucas thinking? He turned to his pea-brained brother. "You've a wife and son to think of, another child on the way. You're not going up against a bunch of street fighters, regardless of what notions of grandeur are swimming around in your empty head."

Lucas observed the group of bare-chested men, who now totalled five, stretching and dancing about the stage. "I'm confident I could handle any of those men."

Anthony threw his hands in the air. "For the love of God, Lucas. This is not your fight."

Bostock tapped his lips in thoughtful contemplation. "I've time to open a book on how long you'll last."

The boy appeared at Mr Bostock's side and handed him a folded note. Clumsy fingers tore open the missive. He read it twice before placing it in the inside pocket of his coat.

"Mr Thorpe said if you step into the ring he will take your case and waive all charges."

"You see," Lucas said smugly. "A round or two and we will have secured Thorpe's services. Bruises heal. Scars fade. There is no need to worry."

"No," Bostock barked. "Mr Thorpe is not referring to you." He faced Anthony with his usual grim expression. "You're to step into the ring. Mr Thorpe needs to know you're a man of conviction. He wants to see if you're a man willing to fight for your life."

CHAPTER 15

Fear should have been the only emotion plaguing Anthony's tense body. While receiving training in the art of pugilism from a young age, as most gentlemen of his ilk were inclined to do, he had never punched with the intention of seriously maiming.

Although now he came to think of it, that was not entirely true.

Upon discovering the man behind the plot to discredit Lucas' name, he had hit him with the power of four years' worth of suppressed anger and frustration.

He had hit to hurt.

The current desire to take vengeance out on any willing party was the motivation behind his sudden eagerness to agree to Thorpe's outrageous demands.

"Tell me you're not considering Thorpe's offer." Lucas' agitated tone penetrated Anthony's thoughts.

Setting foot on the platform would undoubtedly result in a scandal. Gossip was often as debilitating as a bullet to the leg. Then again, Society could forgive a gentleman falling prey to reckless pursuits, more than they could forgive a gentleman for abusing a servant girl and then disposing of the problem.

"This is not the same as friendly sparring in a saloon," Lucas reiterated. "You will be fighting for more than a few words of praise from your tutor."

Indeed, Anthony was fighting for his life—and the lives of every member of his family for years to come.

With a growl of discontent, Lucas turned his attention to Bostock. "My brother has no experience with street brawlers. They fight without rules, lack integrity."

Bostock shrugged. "A hunger to succeed often proves to be the only skill a man needs. These are Thorpe's terms. You can accept, or you can walk away."

Walk away? There was not a place in the world that would protect him should he fail to pay the blackmailer's extortionate fee.

Lucas' expression darkened. "They're the terms of—"

"I agree to the terms," Anthony blurted, astounded by his eagerness for them to beat him until his body was but a rainbow of purple and pink bruises. "I'll step onto the plat-form. I'll last as long as I can. In return, Thorpe will assist me until I am free to sleep peacefully in my bed at night."

Lucas grabbed Anthony's arm so tight he pinched the skin. "Have you lost your mind? So much for protecting your reputation. You will be the topic of conversation in all the clubs tomorrow."

The jeering crowd called out for Brutus the Beast. Their hero. Their saviour. Their chants were like that of an audience at a Roman arena. They roused images of weak men posing as gladiators, waiting behind the iron lattice gate knowing they were but a sword slice away from meeting their maker.

Bostock cleared his throat. "I must insist you take your place on the platform. Now is not the time to concern yourself with gossip. You said you were a man in desperate need and now you have an opportunity to show your determination to win." Bostock stared down the flat bridge of his nose. "Regardless of the cost."

Anthony faced Lucas and opened his hands in a gesture of surrender. "You heard Bostock. I must fight to prove my worth, and that is what I intend to do."

During the months since Emily's death, inadequacy had become Anthony's constant companion. Knowing he had succumbed to blackmail felt as though he was suffering from an incurable disease. The potent poison flowed through him, infecting his mood, tainting his honour, destroying his self-respect.

The sudden pulsing in his fists signalled his body's willingness to fight back. Sucking in a deep breath, he shrugged out of his coat and thrust it at Lucas.

"I need your support, not your criticism." Anthony raised his hand when Lucas opened his mouth to speak. "I need to know you are with me."

Lucas shook his head. "Of course I'm bloody well with you. That does not mean I have to like what you're about to do."

"Then you can make yourself useful and ensure no one steals my clothes." Anthony hoped an element of humour would wipe the frown from his brother's brow.

Anthony stripped down to his breeches. There was something unrefined, primitive, even savage, about baring one's body in public.

Lucas' gaze travelled over the breadth of his chest. "I believe there is something else you have neglected to tell me. A man does not have such a finely developed torso unless he is used to manual labour. Did you give your gardeners notice?"

Hoping to discover the identity of Emily's murderer had forced him to work on his strength and stamina. Riding, fencing, a few hours chopping wood, had all helped to build a more muscular physique. "Why waste money on labour when I can do the job of two men?"

"It's time." Bostock gripped Anthony's bare shoulder and forced him to face his opponents. Meaty fingers pressed into his skin. "A swift uppercut to the jaw will take out any one of these men. Don't dance around them. Look for the opening and take a shot."

"Which one of these charming fellows is Brutus the Beast?" Lucas asked.

Bostock gestured to the slight figure entering the room. He was a good half a foot shorter than the average man, appeared even more so when compared to the hefty stature of his opponents. Brutus was neither a brute nor a beast. Indeed, he had the body frame of a youth of fourteen. Every rib protruded through his thin silvery skin. Anthony's initial reaction was relief until he noted Lucas' look of horror.

"Good Lord," Lucas gasped. "Whatever you do, give Brutus a wide berth. He'll be as nippy as a terrier. You'll not see his punches until they connect with your jaw."

Anthony nodded. He just wanted to get it over with, hoped that a few scrapes and bruises would be the limit of his injuries.

"Keep your back to the crowd," Bostock said. "Pick one man and Brutus will take care of the rest."

A tense silence descended on the room when Anthony stepped onto the platform. Numerous comments pierced the moment of stillness. Who the hell had let the nabob fight? Where was The Piper? The whispers soon became cheers as the semi-secretive community pushed aside their distrust to embrace the newcomer.

Anthony took the corner nearest Bostock. He scanned the opposition. Minus Brutus, there were five men. It was not difficult to imagine they were the gentlemen on his list of suspects. Focusing on the burly oaf nearest to him, or the Earl of Barton in his mind, Anthony clenched his fists ready to make someone pay for his misfortune.

The clang from a large handbell echoed through the room. A deep snarling growl emanated from the depths of the oaf's throat and he turned to face Anthony.

"The Fancy's mine." The oaf bared his black teeth to his fellow opponents. Saliva foamed at the corners of his mouth. Seemingly, they all considered Anthony an easy target.

With his fists held high, Anthony kept a defensive stance. It was imperative he ignored the boisterous antics of the crowd, and the heavy thud of a dead weight hitting the stage as Brutus knocked the first man to the floor.

The oaf shuffled closer, his soulless eyes conveying a fierce hunger to win. He took a swing at Anthony with his mallet-like claw, then another, and another.

Both fencing and riding required agility, and so it was not difficult to avoid the cumbersome attack. With lightning speed, Anthony slid to the left, found an opening and jabbed the oaf twice in the ribs. As expected, the man shifted his guard to favour his weaker side and so Anthony slid to the right and delivered another round of brutal blows.

Despite Bostock and Lucas shouting instructions, Anthony chose to listen to his instincts. He'd wanted to knock the Earl of Barton's teeth down his throat. The oaf would act as the substitute.

After dodging a few more mistimed attacks, Anthony saw an opening. He took the shot, threw his body weight into the punch that connected with the jaw. With flailing arms, the oaf stumbled back off the platform to a round of boos and heckles.

With a quick shake of the head to focus his attention, Anthony realised there were only three other men left on the platform. Two contenders were attempting to tackle Brutus. If they took the favourite out, then they had a better chance of winning.

Feeling a sudden rush of energy, Anthony approached the group, picking the plumper of the two to taunt until the man had no choice but to turn and fight.

Despite his slow movements, the rather rotund fellow possessed some skill. Indeed, Anthony took an unexpected blow to the stomach, one to the ribs. He gasped, gulped to replace the air knocked out of his lungs.

"God damn it, move!" Lucas shouted. "Keep your guard up. Don't give him another chance to hit you."

Anthony inhaled through his nose, tightened his abdominal muscles, kept his weight on the balls of his feet. Again, he was going to have to use agility to overcome the precise punches. He ducked, moved, jabbed at the barrel of fat that concealed the man's ribs. He waited for an opening, released a succession of rapid punches that split the skin on his knuckles and sent his opponent tumbling from the platform.

And then there were two.

Brutus was the only other man left in the ring.

Anthony dabbed the back of his hand on his breeches to soak up the blood. Once again, there was a moment of silence while the spectators caught their breath, too.

Brutus gave a cheeky grin. "I've never met a Fancy pluck enough to come to the scratch," he said, though the words hardly made any sense.

"I need to prove my worth," Anthony replied.

Brutus inclined his head. "And I need to feed my family."

A feeling of mutual respect passed between them. They took their positions, raised their fists. And Anthony moved gingerly forward.

The beast was light on his feet. Quick reflexes prevented Anthony from landing a punch. The beast's succession of swift movements made one feel slightly disoriented, caused a lack of focus.

Just as Lucas predicted, Anthony failed to notice Brutus' punch until it landed on his cheek. His head vibrated from the shock. Still stunned, the second punch came up to connect just below the chin to take Anthony clean off his feet.

Lights flickered in Anthony's eyes as he lay stretched out on the wooden boards. His vision blurred. The crowd's cheers sounded muffled. Somewhere in the distance, he could hear Lucas calling out to him. And then he slipped down into the dark depths of unconsciousness.

CHAPTER 16

"Surely they should be home by now." Sarah moved to the window and parted the drapes. She rubbed the fine layer of mist from the pane and gazed out at the deserted street.

"I do not suppose Mr Thorpe is an easy man to find," Helena replied.

Sarah glanced back over her shoulder to where Helena was sitting in the chair near the fire. "Did you note Mrs Chambers' expression when we told her that Mr Thorpe would be making enquiries, too?"

Helena chuckled. "They are obviously acquainted. While she praised his work, I sensed an element of disquiet. I imagine there is a certain rivalry between them. A lady working in a man's world would have something to prove."

Mrs Chambers was not at all what they had expected. One would imagine a female enquiry agent to be a stern-faced spinster who wore dull dresses to convey a thorough dislike for fun and frivolities. On the contrary, the lady oozed an inherent feminine appeal, a mysterious aura that captured one's attention. No doubt Mrs Chambers had a whole host of admirers vying for her company.

"I liked her." Sarah turned back to the window. "She has a way of instilling confidence in her ability to get the job done. I just hope Lord Harwood is not angry that we took matters into our own hands."

"Well, we cannot pin all our hopes on Mr Thorpe. And despite believing they are men of modern times, I know Lucas would doubt Mrs Chambers' suitability for enquiry work."

"Do you think we should have told her about the circumstances surrounding Emily Compton's death?"

"For now, we need her to focus on establishing the whereabouts of the gentlemen on the list." Helena sighed. "It will be Anthony's decision to tell her more."

The sound of horses' hooves pounding the cobblestones captured Sarah's attention. She pressed her face to the glass. The golden glare of a carriage lamp appeared in the grey misty gloom.

"They're back." A frisson of excitement rippled through her as she watched the footman rush to open the carriage door. Just the thought of gazing upon Anthony's handsome face made her feel all light and giddy.

Mr Dempsey stepped out first. He turned back, grabbed Lord Harwood's elbow and helped him to descend the three metal steps.

Fear gripped her by the throat to obliterate all pleasant emotions.

"Something is wrong." The tremble in Sarah's voice echoed the sudden sense of panic rising in her chest. "Something has happened to Lord Harwood."

Sarah stood frozen to the spot. Immobile. Incapable of moving a muscle. All her dreams crumbled to dust before her eyes. Was he hurt? Was he injured? Had they been accosted by footpads whilst roaming the back streets of Whitechapel?

"What do you mean something is wrong?" Helena asked.

Sarah swung around upon hearing the solemn clip of footsteps on the tiled floor in the hallway. She stared at the door, not knowing what to expect.

The butler appeared first and then stepped aside as Anthony and Mr Dempsey entered the drawing room.

Helena shot out of the chair; her sudden gasp heightened Sarah's fragile nerves.

"Good Lord." Helena rushed forward, raised a trembling hand to Anthony's cheek but left it shaking in mid-air. "What has happened to your face?"

Anthony dabbed his cheek with the tips of his fingers. His knuckles were cut, the skin raw. Bright pink blotches were tinged with claret-coloured blood.

Mr Dempsey cleared his throat. "Would you like the good news or the bad news?"

"The bad," Helena blurted. "Tell me the bad. Were you robbed? Were you attacked on your way to find Mr Thorpe?"

Mr Dempsey shook his head. "Anthony was one of seven men who took part in a boxing match at a house in Marylebone."

"Boxing?" Helena blinked rapidly. "Why would you be boxing when you went out to find Mr Thorpe?"

"It was not through choice." Anthony flexed his jaw and winced. "Does anyone mind if I sit down?"

"Heavens." Helena stepped out of the way and gestured to the sofa. "Are you hurt? Are you in any pain?"

Anthony shook his head as he flopped down into the seat. "No. I'm simply exhausted. It's been years since I fought one man let alone three."

Sarah stared at the purple bruise gracing Anthony's cheek.

Her fingers covered her mouth. Fear prevented her from moving or speaking. Their gazes locked. He gave a weak smile and nodded. The silent communication was perhaps a way of reassuring her all was well.

Still, her heart thumped wildly in her chest.

Mr Dempsey waited for them to sit before taking a seat on the sofa. "Mr Thorpe agreed to take the case on the condition Anthony fought in the ring with a group of street brawlers."

Helena sat perched on the edge of the chair. "And you accepted these barbaric terms?"

"What choice did I have?" Anthony shrugged. A weak smile touched his lips. "I was one of the last men standing. Unfortunately, a fellow by the name of Brutus the Beast knocked me unconscious with a killer punch."

"Brutus the Beast?" Helena gasped. "I can only imagine how terrifying that must have been."

"But you are not injured?" Sarah managed to find her voice. "You have not suffered any permanent damage?"

"No, Miss Roxbury. Everything is working just as it ought."

"His reputation has taken a blow," Lucas said in jest. "When people associate scandal with the name Dempsey, they will no longer be referring to me."

Helena tutted. "Is that why you look so pleased when an ugly black bruise mars your poor brother's face?"

Mr Dempsey patted Anthony on the back. "I don't think I have ever been more proud of him. There is nothing as honourable as a man fighting for a cause."

"But Anthony detests violence."

"Not anymore." Lucas chuckled. "You have not seen his toned physique. I believe he has been preparing for the event for some time."

A delightful image of a muscular torso flitted into Sarah's

mind. She wondered what it would be like to caress the chis-elled contours. Would his skin feel like silk shrouding hard stone? Would he radiate an inherently masculine power that would render her helpless?

Helpless.

The word forced her to acknowledge her feelings. Panic sought to destroy the faint flicker of desire. What would she do if she lost him?

Sarah gripped the arms of the chair. "You … you could have been killed," she said, struggling to keep a rein on her emotions. "People have been known to fall ill days after a blow to the head. They go to sleep and never wake up."

"Trust me. My blood is pumping so quickly I doubt I'll be able to sleep for a week." Anthony's intense gaze searched her face. "Besides, it suddenly occurs to me that I have too much to live for."

"Miss Roxbury has a point," Mr Dempsey said, his tone a little more solemn. "You should not be home alone. Indeed, perhaps you should at least attempt to stay awake for a few more hours. You will stay here the night. We shall take it in turns to keep you company."

"I am not a child, Lucas. I do not need coddling. I've taken a punch to the jaw not a mallet to the head."

"You're right. A child you are most certainly not." Mr Dempsey stretched his arms behind his head and yawned. "After what I witnessed this evening, you are a man in every sense of the word. But you should know, my reasons for wanting to keep you here are purely selfish."

"Don't tell me. Should I meet my demise, the thought of being a viscount fills you with dread and loathing."

"Indeed." Mr Dempsey chuckled. "If anything should happen to you, I shall be forced to take a seat in the House of

Lords. And you know how much I despise pomp and ceremony."

❧

Mr Dempsey escorted a tired-looking Helena to their chamber. They agreed that Sarah would sit with Anthony for an hour in the drawing room until Mr Dempsey returned to keep a watchful eye on his brother.

"Are you warm enough?" Anthony said as he poked and prodded the fire with the metal rod. "I can add more coal if necessary."

"No. I'm fine." Why would she need the heat from the fire when her body burned at the thought of being alone with him? "But you should be resting, not tending to my needs."

"I have no need to rest. My mind is calm and at ease. Strangely, I have never felt more invigorated."

"Well, it does not hurt to be cautious." Sleep would elude her tonight. The fear of living without him would haunt her, rousing unwanted images of waking to discover dreadful news. "Perhaps a drink will relax you a little, help with any pain."

A drink would certainly settle her nerves.

Sarah examined the decanters on the drinks tray, pulled the stoppers and sniffed for there were no silver labels draped around the crystal vessels.

Anthony moved to stand at her side. Had someone covered her eyes with a blindfold, she would have known the moment he came within a few feet. Something happened to the air around them. It pulsed with an intense energy that saw fit to rob one of breath and all rational thought.

"I think you'll find they are both brandy of a sort," he

said. His arm brushed against hers as he leant forward and picked up a decanter. "This one is cognac."

"Having three sisters, I am not a connoisseur of gentlemen's spirits."

He poured the cognac into a glass and held it up to her. "Take a sip. Tell me what you taste. Do any unusual flavours tingle on your tongue?"

She thought to decline. But there was something about the way he spoke, with a smooth, rich drawl that made her put the glass to her lips.

He watched with interest, his blue eyes alight with pleasure as she held the amber liquid in her mouth before swallowing.

Flames scorched her throat. "Good heavens." She almost choked as she sucked in a breath. Panting proved to be the only way to cool her mouth.

"I said a sip, not a mouthful." He pursed his lips. "I doubt you were able to taste a thing. Are you all right?"

"Yes. Yes." She thrust the glass back at him. "It was just a little more potent than I expected. But I did taste something."

"What?"

"Fire."

A chuckle burst from his lips. "Don't make me laugh. My cheek aches whenever I flex my jaw. I've not dared to look in the mirror for it feels as though the swelling covers my entire face."

The purple bruise was tinged with black flecks. It ran at an angle along his cheekbone. Sarah reached out to him, her hand hovering over the mark as though she had the power to heal.

"It is not as bad as that. But I think your bruise makes you look rather scandalous. It speaks of mischief and utter impropriety."

"Are you saying you find something appealing about disgrace?" He swallowed what was left in the glass and placed it back on the table.

"I find something appealing about you, regardless of all else." Her gaze fell to his mouth, focused on the small mark cutting into his bottom lip. "You should let me put some ointment on that cut."

"And why would I let you do that?"

"Why?" His response took her by surprise. "Because it will help it to heal."

A mischievous grin played at the corners of his mouth. He closed the small gap between them and took hold of her chin. "Why would I want to do anything that would prevent me from kissing you?"

Hot blood raced through her body far too quickly, the sudden rush rising until she could feel her face glowing. "If it hurts to laugh, I suspect it will pain you far more to kiss me."

"I have recently come to accept that nothing will prevent me from enjoying the taste of your lips." He lowered his head, brushed his mouth softly over hers. "If tonight has taught me anything, it's that I'm rather partial to the illicit, although there is nothing immoral about the way I feel about you."

Her heart lurched. "You know what happened the last time we were intimate," she said as he rained kisses along her jaw.

"You will have to remind me," he drawled as his arm snaked around her back to pull her closer.

"We are liable to lose our heads, Anthony. I cannot—" She paused as he ran the pad of his thumb over her bottom lip. "I cannot fight the hunger that consumes me. I cannot stop the longing that writhes deep inside. I cannot—"

"Hush." He put his finger to her lips. "Don't fight it. We

belong together. Trust me. Let me love you like I want to. Despite my improper behaviour where you are concerned, know that I will always honour and protect you."

She wanted this man more than she had ever wanted anything her entire life. And she did trust him. He was not the sort of gentleman to partake in meaningless affairs. He was not a cad or a scoundrel.

"I could have lost you tonight," she said, purely to placate her conscience. She needed some justification, a reason to explain why she was about to give herself to him. "When I think of you lying cold and alone, my body trembles with fear."

"Then let me make you tremble for an entirely different reason." Anthony cupped her cheek. "I am very much alive. Touch me. Feel the warmth of my skin on your palm. I'll not leave you, Sarah. Where ever you go, I shall follow."

Love filled her chest. The feeling eradicated all doubts. "Then I want to give myself to you. I want to show you what you mean to me. I want you to show me what it is to love with my body."

"It would be my pleasure," he whispered as he lowered his head to claim her mouth.

Only one thought drifted through her mind before she became lost in the dizzying heights of desire.

When it came to Anthony Dempsey, everything felt right.

CHAPTER 17

*A*s a man who had never experienced the dark, murky realms of unconsciousness, Anthony found the event had resulted in an epiphany of sorts. An awakening. A way of seeing the world stripped of its restraints.

He wanted Sarah Roxbury—that was nothing new.

Only now he was willing to do whatever was necessary to fulfil his dream — which was why he could not tear his mouth from hers even though he knew it would result in their complete surrender.

Good God. He would never grow tired of her sweet taste, of the way her soft body moulded to his. For the first time in his life, securing his heritage for future generations seemed more than appealing. Furthering his bloodline was now far from a chore.

His brother would have no fear of inheriting. Anthony doubted he would leave Sarah Roxbury's bed once they were married.

The woman soon to be his wife chose that moment to moan into his mouth, to press her sumptuous breasts against his chest and partake in a slow seductive dance.

Bloody hell!

Anthony was known for his steely reserve. But even a monk would crumble under the strain of temptation. *Strain* was indeed the appropriate word. His manhood swelled and throbbed against his breeches in a desperate attempt to break free.

He tore his lips away to catch his breath, to give her an opportunity to gather her thoughts.

"This is going exactly as you feared," he panted as his traitorous hands settled on her buttocks to draw her against the throbbing evidence of his arousal. "If you do not wish to continue, you must say so now."

Respect and honour were codes he had always lived by. But he could think of nothing other than settling between her soft thighs and driving home.

She blinked rapidly. "All I know is how wonderful it feels to be with you."

"Do you understand where this will lead if you continue to kiss me in the same wanton way?" He did not want to sound condescending, but he had to make her understand the consequences of their actions.

"What wanton way?" She looked up at him, her blue eyes swimming with desire. He could not help but kiss her once more on the mouth. "If ... if loving you means I behave a little recklessly then so be it."

Reckless did not even begin to define the nature of his thoughts.

"If we continue, then there can be only one outcome. Our lives will be forever entwined."

Sarah sighed. "Not only is that the least romantic way of suggesting marriage, but your dire tone is ruining the moment." She raised herself up on her toes and kissed him to the point he almost forgot his own name. "There, that is better. Now can you please lock the door and try not to deter me from what I imagine will the most magnificent experience of my entire life?"

"Magnificent?" he said as he strode over to the door and turned the key in the lock. He tried the handle a few times just to be sure. "What chance have I of meeting such high expectations? Perhaps I should warn you it has been some time since—"

"Stop talking, Anthony. Come here and kiss me again."

What man would dare refuse such an enticing invitation?

"And do hurry," she continued in the voice of a skilled courtesan. "I estimate we have but fifty minutes before your brother returns."

Under usual circumstances, it would prove to be plenty of time. But he suspected he would need hours to worship Sarah as she deserved. Besides, knowing the train of Lucas' thoughts, he would not return to the drawing room until he heard Miss Roxbury climb the stairs and enter her bedchamber.

It took but a second for him to cross the room and return to the comfort of her arms. Despite the serious nature of their conversation, once their mouths met, desire ignited like a blazing inferno.

Sarah's frantic hands pushed his coat from his shoulders. Anthony suppressed a groan, for his ribs were sore and tender. The muscles in his arms ached. The bruise on his cheek throbbed. But he would be damned before he would stop.

"Here allow me." In his eagerness to be free from all constraints, he tore at his waistcoat. A gold button fell to the floor and rolled under the sofa. As he tugged on his cravat, he stopped abruptly. His mouth fell open. His chin touched his chest as he watched Sarah slip off her shoes and fiddle with her dress.

All he could do was stand motionless and stare.

"You could at least help me with my buttons," she complained.

"Of course." Anthony threw his cravat to the floor, dragged his shirt over his head and dropped it onto the pile of discarded garments.

Sarah sucked in a sharp breath. With wide eyes, her gaze travelled over his chest. "Your brother certainly has the measure of you." When it dipped to the waistband of his breeches, his manhood jerked in response.

"Turn around and let me help you out of your clothing," he said with some amusement. "At present, you have an unfair advantage."

"Oh, must I? I rather like the view."

"Do you want help with your buttons or not?"

There had been a few magical moments in his life: the day he had learned his brother had married the woman who'd saved him. An event equalled by the birth of his nephew. Undressing the woman who had claimed his heart proved to be as fulfilling, though he imagined joining with her would surpass all else.

Damn.

He could not stop his fingers from shaking as he fumbled with the buttons. Helping her out of her dress, petticoat and stays, he stepped back as she turned to face him. His deepest, darkest desire stood before him in nothing but her chemise, the tips of her nipples protruding through the fine material.

His mouth was dry, his throat parched.

She clasped her hands, held her arms nervously in front of her to hide her body.

"There is no need to be shy," he said as he stepped forward and took her hands in his. "Not with me."

"I expected to be cold, but I'm not." Biting her bottom lip, she glanced at the door. "But what if someone should come down to check on you?"

"You're wearing nothing but a chemise." He swallowed deeply at the mere thought of what treasures lay hidden beneath the thin cotton. "I'm hardly going to open the door and let them in. Besides, no one will disturb us."

The smile gracing her lips warmed his heart. "Should we not blow out the candles?"

"Love, I have waited a month for the pleasure of seeing you like this. Indeed, never in my wildest imagination would I have believed this moment possible. Let me look upon you as I have longed to do."

A blush crept up to colour her cheeks. "Then you must find a way to bolster my courage."

The only way to settle her nerves was to heighten her pleasure. With that in mind, he claimed her mouth. Their tongues tangled, partook in an erotic dance, the steps utterly unique. Anthony teased a moan from her lips, took it as a sign to be bold.

Through the layer of fine fabric, he touched her intimately, found the sweet spot between her thighs. He massaged and caressed until she pressed against his hand, until her chest heaved and she struggled to stand still.

With his lips locked with hers, he gathered the material of her undergarment, bunched it up to her waist and slid his fingers into her slick flesh.

"*Anthony.*" His name burst from her lips.

The seductive scent of her arousal was his undoing, yet he continued to pleasure her until she gasped for breath. Both her hands gripped his shoulders for balance. The sharp nails digging into his skin heightened his pleasure. Her head fell back. Golden curls escaped from the pins to fall in waves down her back.

He had never seen such a glorious sight.

And then her release was upon her. She clung to him as her body shuddered. Moan after sweet moan filled his head as he pushed inside her with his fingers.

Bloody hell.

She felt hot and wet.

She felt divine.

Scandal was now his new name.

He did not want to wait for the tremors to subside. "Forgive my rather crass approach, but would you prefer the floor or the sofa?" Impatience was evident in his tone.

She lifted her head, opened her glazed eyes and stared at him with a look of wonder. "I don't care. You choose."

A raw carnal need took over. He wanted to cover her with his body. He wanted the space to give her everything he had.

"Then let us lie before the fire." He took the ends of her chemise and dragged the garment over her head before she could protest. For a moment, breathing proved to be a problem as he gazed upon her luscious form.

"Is … is there something wrong?" she said when he failed to speak.

"Lord, no. I do not think I have laid eyes on anything more beautiful in my entire life."

Her cheeks glowed at the compliment. A mischievous smile played at the corners of her mouth. "Now I find I am the one at a disadvantage."

He looked down at his breeches. "You want me to remove them?"

"I know I am a novice when it comes to intimate relations, but I'm certain that is the idea."

"Then I do not wish to disappoint." With their gazes locked, he yanked off his boots and stockings, undid the buttons and side buckle until his breeches hung low at the hips. "I should tell you that I do not favour drawers. The way I feel about you will be clearly evident—"

"Do not say any more. Let me see for myself."

Feigning an air of arrogance, he pushed the garment to the floor and stepped out of it to stand as naked as the day he was born.

Wide eyes journeyed over him from head to toe. They lingered on his jutting erection. "My, you must admire me a great deal."

"As I am sure you're now aware, my feelings for you are fairly substantial."

"Indeed."

He gestured to the floor next to the fire. "Shall we continue?"

"Most definitely. Though I do have some reservations as to how this will work."

"Trust me." He held his hand out to her. "It will work exceedingly well."

Once again, she came into his arms. He lowered her down, covered her delectable body with his own. The kiss they shared spoke of something far deeper than a desire for pleasure. When he entered her body and pushed past her virginity, he truly did give her everything he had to give.

He gave her his heart.

He gave her his soul.

With each slow, measured thrust he let her feel the depth of his devotion. It did not take long for their passion to overwhelm them. Instinctively, Sarah gripped him tightly with her soft thighs and rocked with him to the tune of their erotic dance.

Wave upon pleasurable wave carried them. As he drove harder, as his thrusts grew more frantic, he knew there was yet one more decision for her to make.

"Do … do you wish me to withdraw?" He panted the words, tried to focus his mind while he waited for her answer.

Two tiny furrows appeared between her brows. Then realisation dawned. She did not take any time to think. "The choice is yours. I trust you, Anthony. I would not be here if I did not believe we had a future."

His rational mind, which currently amounted to nothing more than a fleeting thought, told him not to behave more recklessly than he had already. However, his need to love Sarah unconditionally reassured him that nothing would stand in the way of him making her his.

With the decision made, he claimed her mouth and pushed slowly into her core. The heavenly experience banished all doubts. Joining with her eased all his pain.

A delightful hum resonated in the back of her throat. To encourage his rhythmical movements, she grabbed his buttocks and rubbed against him. His thrusts were deeper, harder, less measured. From her breathless pants, he knew she was but a second or two from completion.

"Anthony," she cried, and he was forced to kiss her to muffle the succession of blissful moans.

When his release came upon him, it was without question the most satisfying experience of his life. Against all sense and reason, he did not withdraw.

It was foolish.

Bloody irresponsible.

But Sarah Roxbury would be his wife. She would be the mother of his children. She would be his friend, his lover, his companion. The only woman who would ever command his complete surrender.

CHAPTER 18

*M*rs Reed lifted the lids on the silver serving dishes lined up on the buffet table and examined the contents. She turned to Mr Dempsey. "Shall I ask Cook to make more eggs, sir?"

Mr Dempsey glanced around the table and raised a brow in enquiry. "By your silence, I assume you've all eaten sufficiently."

"I am completely satisfied." A smile touched Anthony's lips as he caught Sarah's gaze. "Even so, I suspect I shall be famished again by supper."

One could not mistake the veiled message within his words. Indeed, Sarah's pulse quickened at the prospect of spending the evening enveloped in his arms.

Her cutlery clattered on the china plate as she attempted to quell the sudden rush of excitement. "Thank you, but I could not manage another morsel."

It felt strange sitting opposite him in such a formal setting. All she wanted to do was slide onto his lap, kiss him and run her fingers through his hair. Their amorous interlude should have soothed the desperate need clawing away inside. But it only served to inflame the deep sense of longing.

Helena cleared her throat. "If we have all finished our meal there is something we must discuss. It is probably best to come straight to the point." She raised her chin. "While you were out searching for Mr Thorpe, Sarah and I also went out."

Mr Dempsey's expression grew dark, ominous. "You went out alone at night?" He threw his napkin onto the table. "You promised me you would stay at home. Damn it, Helena, the streets are no place for unaccompanied women."

Helena reclined back in the chair. "I promised we would not follow you in your search for Mr Thorpe. That is all. Besides, we took the carriage. Jackson waited. He brought us straight back home. We were in no danger."

Anthony's stern expression revealed he was just as furious.

"We meant to tell you last night," Sarah said in an effort to placate him. "But we were distracted by your injuries from the boxing match. It was never our intention to deceive you."

"Where did you go?" Anthony stared at her beneath hooded lids.

Sarah met his gaze. "To Madame Fontaine's."

"Madame Fontaine's!" Mr Dempsey cried. "Please tell me it is not a house of ill repute."

Helena's eyes grew wide. "Of course not. What business would we have in such a place? No. It is a modiste's shop on New Bond Street."

Mr Dempsey sighed. "Your need for a new dress forced you to go out at night? Is the woman so popular she cannot see you during the day?"

"You were in town for a matter of hours. I doubt a modiste on New Bond Street would offer appointments at such short notice." Suspicion marred Anthony's tone. "So why would you go there?"

"Well, it seemed ludicrous to pin all our hopes on finding Mr Thorpe." Helena picked a piece of toast from the rack and began slathering it in butter. "So we thought we would hire an enquiry agent of our own."

Anthony jumped to his feet. "You did what?"

Sarah swallowed deeply. "We hired Mrs Chambers to investigate the gentlemen you said attended the party at Elton Park." Her throat felt tight to the point it was hard to breathe. "She met us at the modiste. Indeed, we are to meet with her again tomorrow."

Anthony shook his head. He placed his hands flat on the table, his penetrating glare as hard as flint. "What did you tell her?"

"Only that we needed to know the whereabouts of all the gentlemen mentioned. We also asked to be notified of their movements over the last few months," Helena informed. "Mrs Chambers knows Emily Compton died leaving a son, but has not been apprised of all the details."

"Do you realise how many fakes and frauds are working in this field?" Anthony exhaled deeply, but the action did little to smooth the creases from his brow. "They know what to say to secure your business. They know how to dupe you into believing they have the skills necessary to help you."

"Do not speak to us as though we are fools," Helena countered. "We were not to know you would find Mr Thorpe or that you would be beaten black and blue by a brute in order to enlist his help."

Helena had the ability to make a person feel foolish without a direct insult.

Anthony sucked in his cheeks. "Mr Thorpe is not so desperate for work that he advertises in the newspaper."

A smile lit up Helena's face. "Neither is Mrs Chambers."

Anthony mumbled under his breath and dropped into the chair. Sarah struggled to hold his gaze but refused to look away. They had done what they thought was best under the circumstances.

"How did you know where to find this woman?" At least Mr Dempsey sounded somewhat calm.

"Lord Banbury gave me her calling card," Helena replied. "It seems his friend, Lady Fanshaw, has used Mrs Chambers' services on a number of occasions."

"I do not want my business bandied about the ballrooms by gossiping matrons." Anthony's eyes were an ice-cold blue as he focused on Helena. He brushed his hand through his hair. "You should have spoken to me before charging off on a fool's errand."

Good Lord.

Sarah sucked in a breath. His sharp tone cut to the bone. Of course, fear formed the basis of his anger. Even so, she felt the need to defend their decision.

"Well, the results will speak for themselves, my lord." Sarah stressed the use of formal address as she knew it would irritate him. "We shall see which one of the agents uncovers the proof you need."

"I know my wife will kick me in the shin for saying this," Mr Dempsey began, "but I do not see how a woman can be a match for a man in that regard. In their line of work they must find themselves in many dangerous situations."

"You should be grateful you are sitting at the end of the table, else you might feel more than a pain in your leg," Helena retorted though her tone carried a hint of humour. "Whilst we are on the topic of confessions"—she paused —"we must also tell you that, while at Elton Park, we entered the cottage and made our own examination of the scene."

The declaration was met with shocked silence.

The air grew heavy, tense. It proved to be stifling, almost suffocating.

Anthony dragged his hand down his face. "I am at a loss for words."

"It is not fair to shut us out, Anthony," Helena said calmly.

"You cannot apprise us of the gory details and not expect us to be inquisitive," Sarah added.

Mr Dempsey sat back and folded his arms across his chest. "But you left Elton Park while we were still searching the cottage."

Sarah chose to answer as she could not let Helena take all the blame. "We visited the cottage while you were occupied in the study."

"But that is impossible. You did not have the key." Anthony tapped the breast pocket of his coat as if he still kept the key there.

Sarah glanced discreetly at Helena, but before she could speak, Mr Dempsey said, "O'Brien taught Helena how to unlock a door using nothing more than a few hairpins. What can I say? It seemed like a good idea at the time."

Again, the room plunged into a morbid silence.

"What you saw in the cottage," Anthony eventually said though his tone was solemn, his expression grave, "it is not something a lady should have to witness. It was never my intention to exclude you. As always, my motivation is to protect. It is what I have been raised to do. By no means does it bear any reflection on your ability to help."

All feelings of anger and frustration melted away. Sarah's heart ached to soothe him. Anthony looked so lost. The gravity of his situation has taken its toll, she realised. Most of the time he was able to suppress his anguish. But the pain was now clear for all to see.

She sat there, helpless, words being the only way to ease the torment etched on his face. "Any other lady would have appreciated your gallant effort," she said. "But you have known Helena long enough to understand that she would also do anything to protect her family." Sarah thought of Prudence, her younger sisters and grandfather. They meant the world to her, too. She felt just as passionate about their welfare and safety. "Family is everything. The need to nurture and protect is not specific to one gender. I would do anything to help you, my lord. Surely everyone around this table knows it, too. Let me try."

A sudden wave of raw emotion rose to the surface, and she covered her mouth as a means to suppress it.

Anthony stared at her—the man who was now her lover and friend. The man who had made it clear he would be her husband. The sadness consuming him moments earlier lifted. Now, his eyes swam with the look of admiration and respect she much preferred.

"We are to meet Mr Thorpe tomorrow to see how he progresses with the investigation." Anthony cast his brother a sidelong glance. "If Lucas has no objection, you may both accompany us there."

Mr Dempsey shrugged. "I hate to think what we'd discover upon our return if we left them behind."

Helena smiled. "You never know, we might be able to offer some insight regarding the scene at the cottage."

"I doubt it." Anthony took a sip of his tea but winced as it must surely be cold. "I have searched the rooms on more than one occasion. Other than the obvious evidence, I found nothing untoward."

"Nothing?" Sarah said coyly. "You mean you did not

wonder about the crystal glasses? You did not find the letter? You did not note that Emily's undergarments were silk or question why they were torn and strewn across the floor?"

"There was a letter?" Anthony's teacup clattered on the saucer. "I searched the drawers and found nothing."

"When a woman receives a note declaring love, she does not hide it in a drawer," Helena said, "unless she is married, and the letter is not from her husband."

Resting his elbow on the table, Anthony rubbed his forehead. "You're saying you found such a letter in the cottage? But where?"

"If your lover sent you a note, Miss Roxbury," Helena said with a smirk, "where would you keep it?"

Even though Sarah knew where they had found the incriminating missive, still her mind drifted back to the night she hugged Isaac Newton's book to her chest and drifted off into a peaceful slumber. It was the closest thing to hugging the man who'd left the gift.

"I would keep it close. Somewhere I could reach for it as I lay in my bed at night. I would read it over and over, inhale the smell of the paper in the hope his scent lingered there. It would be the last thing I looked at before bed. Upon waking, it would be the first thing I reached for."

"You found it under her pillow?" Anthony said.

Sarah nodded. "It was hidden in the cotton case, though I must warn you that we cannot assume it is genuine. Indeed, Mrs Chambers is certain she can verify its authenticity."

"You gave Mrs Chambers the letter?"

"We did. It was signed by a gentleman named James," Helena said. "Of course, now we know of those on your list of guests, the obvious conclusion would be that Mr James St. John was her lover."

"But you do not believe that to be the case?" Mr Dempsey asked.

"I know nothing is as it seems. There are too many things that do not make sense," Helena replied. "For instance, where is the decanter or the bottle used to fill the glasses? Why tear the undergarments? Did Emily have two lovers vying for her attention?"

Trying to come up with the correct answer to the various questions hurt Sarah's head. "I eagerly await Mrs Chambers' opinion." She turned to Anthony. "Assuming you grant permission for us to inform her of the exact nature of Emily Compton's death."

"What is your opinion of the woman's character, Miss Roxbury? Do you trust Mrs Chambers?"

Mrs Chambers had a commanding, authoritative presence. Yet, they had glimpsed a softer side, a kind compassionate nature she hid beneath a hard shell. Sarah knew instinctively that the woman was both trustworthy and genuine.

"My feeling is that Mrs Chambers is a consummate professional who will employ meticulous methods to achieve results," Sarah informed. "So yes, I trust her and have faith in her ability to get the job done."

Anthony's expression was one of thoughtful contemplation. "Then I trust your opinion. You may confide in her. You have my consent to apprise her of all the details."

An overwhelming sense of pride burst to life in Sarah's chest. His willingness to concede showed great strength of character.

"Indeed, the issues you've mentioned regarding the scene at the cottage were not apparent to me," Anthony continued. He met his brother's gaze and through a series of facial expressions and nods communicated silently. "Whilst on the subject of confessions, there is something I have failed to mention."

Sarah straightened her spine. "There can be no more secrets between us." A hint of panic infused her tone.

"I agree." Anthony held her gaze. "The only reason I have withheld information is that it pains me to reveal my shame and weakness in this regard."

Sarah swallowed down the lump in her throat. "This morning has been about revealing truths, offering loyalty and unwavering support. You have no need to fear our judgement."

"Then you should know that I am to spend the rest of the morning at my bank. I am to gather five hundred pounds in order to pay the gentleman who murdered Emily. I'm afraid to say that, for the last four months, I have been the victim of blackmail."

CHAPTER 19

The buildings raced past the carriage window in a blur. Anthony stared out into the distance, lost in thought, as they rattled along the streets on their way to the office of Thorpe & Jones.

Two years had passed since Anthony's first visit to Mr Thorpe. Many things had changed during that time, namely Lucas was now a doting husband and father. However, the most drastic changes had occurred during the last five months.

Brawling with street fighters and succumbing to blackmail were but two of the numerous stains on Anthony's once blemish-free character. But that was not what bothered him the most.

Like the worst of scoundrels, he had taken Sarah Roxbury's virginity on the floor of his brother's drawing room, whilst his family were upstairs no less.

Good Lord. He had been so desperate to have the woman who constantly occupied his thoughts, he'd not been thinking clearly. Even now, all he had to do was recall the moment to experience a sudden rush of lustful longing. Never had carnal cravings monopolised all rational thought.

But was it any way to treat the lady he loved? And he was in love with Sarah, deeply so. That was no longer a question to be bandied back and forth in his fragile mind. A faint chuckle burst from his lips. Despite shame being his constant companion, he was not sorry. When it came to Sarah Roxbury, he would take her any way he could.

"You find something amusing about being stuck behind a herd of cattle on their way to market?" Lucas asked. "Damn, if Carter doesn't jump down and chase them off, I most definitely will."

Anthony blinked numerous times. He'd not realised the carriage had stopped. "There is no room in my addled brain to worry about cows."

"Perhaps not, but you despise being late." Lucas peered out of the window. "I should have shared a carriage with Helena and Miss Roxbury. One word from Jackson and the herd would be charging to market."

With a quick glance at his pocket watch, Anthony shuffled to the edge of the seat. "Let's get out. It's a two-minute walk to Hyde Street."

Despite the fact they were not moving, Anthony rapped twice on the roof. The road might clear at any moment, and he envisaged Lucas hanging on to the open door, his best boots dragged through manure as he clung on for dear life.

Anthony laughed as he stepped out onto the road and conveyed instructions to his coachman.

"For a gentleman with pressing problems you seem rather cheerful this morning," Lucas said as they marched along Bow Street. "Was it your midnight stroll in the garden last night that has left you in such high spirits?"

"You saw us?"

"Us?" A smirk touched Lucas' lips. "You mean you were not alone?"

"You know damn well I was with Miss Roxbury, though surely you have more interesting ways to pass your time than snooping on your houseguests."

Lucas shrugged. "I am a light sleeper. What can I say?" After a brief pause, he said, "I assume you intend to marry her. You are not the sort of gentleman to partake in illicit liaisons with an innocent."

There was no need to answer. Lucas was adept at reading minds.

"Ah, I see," Lucas continued. "You do intend to marry, and Miss Roxbury is no longer innocent."

"You need not sound so smug."

It was Lucas' turn to laugh. "It is a relief to find you are human. I can only imagine what Father would say about your antics were he here. His eldest son parading in public without his shirt, bare-knuckle fighting and relieving an unmarried maiden of her virginity. Heavens, you'd be shipped a little further afield than Boston."

Anthony put his hand to his chest. "Oh, you're so amusing my ribs ache. But if you're worried about my reckless behaviour, then rest assured. I shall marry Miss Roxbury as soon as I've dealt with this mess."

"Helena will be thrilled."

"At least I am not a complete disappointment," Anthony said as they turned into Hyde Street. Stopping to inspect the row of shabby terrace houses, he frowned. "I'd be surprised to learn Thorpe lives here. Considering his line of work, I doubt he would conduct business at his home address."

"A man of his ilk will have access to many properties." Lucas walked on a few strides ahead. He pointed to a brass number on a blue paint-chipped door. "This is the one."

Anthony stared up at the row of sash windows, noting one was nothing more than an image of a frame painted on the brick. They approached the house and were about to knock when Mr Bostock opened the door.

Bostock's small beady eyes scanned Anthony's face. "You were lucky. Most men who fight with Brutus end up with a broken nose."

Anthony inclined his head. "I shall bear that in mind though I doubt I'll have cause to meet him again."

Bostock made an odd puffing sound that Anthony came to realise was a chuckle. "You'd best come inside. Mr Thorpe is waiting."

Bostock stepped to the side, and they squeezed past his bulky frame. There were but three doors leading off the narrow hall.

"You'll find Mr Thorpe in the front room," Bostock informed. "He likes to know the moment his clients arrive."

The room was what one would expect from a drawing room: numerous chairs and side tables placed in an orderly fashion, a landscape painting on one wall, a portrait of a solemn-looking gentleman above the mantel. Thorpe sat in a leather wingback chair near the window, positioned in such a way as to give him an optimum view of the comings and goings on Hyde Street.

Thorpe stood and inclined his head by way of a greeting. The bruise on Anthony's cheek drew his attention. "Trouble seems to find some men. Indeed, it appears to run in the family."

When they'd met Thorpe two years ago, his white wig had aged him far beyond his actual years. He'd lacked the presence of any facial hair. The creases on his face had been applied with some artistry merely as a means to enhance his disguise. Now, his black hair touched his shoulders. Anthony imagined few men had neither the ability nor the desire to grow such an impressive beard. The wrinkles were no more. At a guess, Anthony imagined Thorpe to be on the better side of thirty.

"We found we could not stay away," Lucas replied. "We missed your wit and warm countenance. And we know of no other man as able when it comes to discreet enquiries."

Thorpe waved at the chairs opposite. "Please, sit. I'm afraid Bostock cannot abide tea, and so you may have a brandy if you're so inclined."

"Not for me." Anthony would suffer no distractions when it came to hearing of Thorpe's progress.

Lucas raised his hand and shook his head.

"Then let us get to the matter at hand." Thorpe waited for them to sit and then dropped into the worn chair. He picked up a brown leather folder from the side table.

"Before you start, you should know my wife will be joining us." Lucas glanced out of the window. "She will be here momentarily, accompanied by the lady my brother has chosen to marry."

Anthony did not refute his claim. "The gentleman we seek has already claimed the life of one woman. I will not have my family living in ignorance."

Thorpe was silent for a moment. His narrowed gaze suggested a mind plagued by conflicting thoughts. "Then we must wait. But my manner is often … blunt," he said, placing the folder back on the table. "I will not make allowances for their delicate constitutions."

"Delicate constitutions?" Lucas snorted. "It is obvious you have never met my wife."

The sound of horses' hooves clattering on the cobble-stones captured their attention. The conveyance stopped outside the house.

Bostock appeared at the drawing room door. "Were you expecting someone else?"

Thorpe nodded. "You may permit the ladies entrance." With his usual impassive expression, the gentleman steepled his fingers at his chest, tapped his fingers together while he waited.

"I trust you have had some success in your investigation?" Anthony asked, impatient to know his efforts in the boxing ring had not been for nought.

"Indeed. I'm certain you'll be pleased." Thorpe glanced casually out of the window. Without any warning, he shot forward.

"What is it?" Anthony followed the man's gaze to see a woman exit Lucas' carriage to stand with Sarah and Helena on the pavement.

"Damn it all," Thorpe muttered loud enough for them to hear. It was the first time Anthony had seen the gentleman's calm demeanour ruffled. A deep frown marred his brow. "Would someone like to explain why the hell Mrs Chambers is approaching my front door?"

Lucas cleared his throat. "My wife took it upon herself to employ the lady's services. At the time we had no notion whether we would find you. She felt it judicious to keep one's options open."

The green vein in Thorpe's temple pulsed. "Please tell me you do not expect me to work with her." He flicked his head at the door. Bostock slipped out into the hallway, albeit somewhat awkwardly. "If Mrs Chambers is working your case, then you do not need my assistance."

Anthony could not decide if it was admiration or condescension that infused the gentleman's tone.

"The ladies are enamoured with her," Anthony informed. "I'm afraid that I cannot disappoint them. Equally, you will notice the painful evidence of our bargain marking my face. I fulfilled my part of our agreement. I trust you will do the same."

Thorpe threw himself back in the seat. "Had I known I would be expected to work with Mrs Chambers, I would have retracted my offer."

"Had I known you would flounder at the thought of working with a woman, I would have refused to step onto the platform," Anthony countered. "But it is done now. As a gentleman, I do not expect you to renege."

If a look could turn a man to stone, Anthony would be as cold and hard as any statue gracing a museum.

"Who said I was a gentleman?" Thorpe's words brimmed with cynicism.

Anthony smirked. "One need not be an enquiry agent to know the difference between a man of breeding and one raised on the streets."

The sudden commotion in the hallway proved distracting.

Thorpe's gaze flicked to the door. A weary sigh left his lips. "Then I shall have to hope we reach a speedy conclusion."

Bostock cleared his throat. "The rest of the party have arrived."

Thorpe arched a brow. "Then do not leave them to wait in a draughty hall."

They all stood.

Helena entered the room first, followed by Sarah. They were introduced to Mr Thorpe. Both Anthony and Lucas offered the ladies their seats and moved to stand behind their respective partners.

The tension in the air was palpable.

Thorpe's penetrating stare settled on the lady in the doorway. "Mrs Chambers." He inclined his head. "It has been some time since our paths have crossed."

With all the elegance and grace of a duchess, Mrs Chambers stepped forward. She offered Thorpe her hand. The coy smile playing on her lips suggested she knew the man would be reluctant to grasp her fingers.

With a hard, unforgiving expression, Thorpe brought her hand to within an inch of his mouth.

Mrs Chambers pursed her lips. Her gaze travelled over his hair, down to the full beard and side whiskers. "I suppose this look suits you, though I much prefer you clean shaven. I'm told Mr Thorpe is your current name of choice."

"One must keep an element of privacy in our line of work."

"Indeed."

Thorpe gestured to the only other available chair. "If you would care to sit, we shall proceed with our business."

"Thank you, Mr Thorpe. As ever, you are a gentleman."

The muscle in Thorpe's cheek twitched. Anthony got the distinct impression his annoyance stemmed from more than a simple case of rivalry.

"Now. Regarding the gentlemen mentioned." Thorpe sat in the wingback chair. He looked through his leather folder, removed a piece of paper and handed it to Anthony. "During the last five months, they have all been in London at some time. Mr James St. John left for Calcutta three months hence and has not returned."

Anthony noted the details of St. John's passage to India. Overcome with shame for his ineptitude, he struggled to hold Mr Thorpe's gaze. "I heard talk of his travels, but one cannot place their trust in gossip. After recent events, nothing surprises me."

"Your information confirms my suspicion that the love

letter was not written by James St. John," Mrs Chambers said. "Indeed, someone else wanted to make it appear St. John and Miss Compton were intimate."

"To what letter do you refer?" Thorpe did not look pleased.

"Why, the letter found at the scene."

"My wife found the letter," Lucas said apologetically. "We were only recently made aware of its existence."

Mrs Chambers coughed. "I compared the note with an authentic copy of St. John's handwriting. It was definitely not a match."

Thorpe brushed his hand through his mop of black hair. "In that case, we shall move on." He blinked and shook his head before exhaling deeply through his nose. "I am also inclined to rule Lord Faversham out. He broke his leg—"

"Falling out of his mistress' bed, three months hence." Mrs Chambers appeared somewhat excited by the news. "It failed to heal properly, and he has been bedridden ever since. He told his mother he fell off his horse after it was spooked whilst riding on the Row. Consequently, he insisted on his mother's discretion as no one wants to admit they lack the skills needed to control such a beast." Noting Thorpe's irritated glare, she said, "Forgive me for interrupting. I find the story rather amusing."

"I assume his mother knows nothing of his mistress," Helena said.

"Apparently not. She informed him—"

"Perhaps we should exchange chairs, Mrs Chambers." Thorpe's menacing tone sliced through the air. "Is there any point in me continuing?"

"Of course." Mrs Chambers' beaming smile lit up the room. "I will not speak again."

"Then I live in hope that you're a woman of your word."

The corners of Mr Thorpe's mouth twitched. He turned his attention to Anthony. "Now, one does not have to be a mathematical genius to know that our five suspects have been narrowed down to three. As for—"

Mrs Chambers raised her gloved hand and wiggled her fingers. "Excuse me."

Thorpe sighed. "Can you at least let me finish a sentence? There will be time for questions later."

"But this is—"

"Please wait, Mrs Chambers."

"Forgive me." The lady inclined her head. "You may continue."

"As it will take time to investigate the remaining three suspects," Thorpe said, ignoring his rival's mocking snort. "I suggest you attend the appointment arranged by the blackmailer. Trust me. Come tomorrow we will know his identity."

"You're confident we will catch him?" Anthony asked.

"Of course. Now, Mrs Chambers. Was there something you wanted to say?"

A confident smile graced her lips. "Pay me no heed, Mr Thorpe. You appear to have everything in hand."

A look of suspicion marred Thorpe's brow. "You're certain there is nothing else you wish to add?"

"Quite certain."

"Very well. Lord Harwood will keep his appointment to pay the blackmailer. Now I've been informed of the time and location, Bostock will assist me in attempting to apprehend the villain. You will go alone, Lord Harwood. We do not wish to alert the fellow of our plan."

Lucas groaned. "You cannot expect me to sit at home and—"

"You will accompany Bostock, Mr Dempsey."

Lucas inclined his head respectfully. He appeared more than pleased with his role.

"And what of the ladies?" Mrs Chambers asked sweetly. "How may we be of assistance?"

Thorpe raised a brow. "For fear of causing offence, I shall keep my opinions to myself. But rest assured we will inform you of our progress."

Sarah cleared her throat but said nothing.

Mrs Chambers held an impassive expression as she brushed a lock of ebony hair from her forehead. "Well, do not give us a second thought. I am sure we will find a way to occupy our time."

CHAPTER 20

"I understand you are betrothed." Mrs Chambers patted Sarah's arm as the carriage trundled along New Bond Street. "One does not need the skill of an enquiry agent to know when two people are in love."

"We have yet to make an announcement," Anthony replied from his seat on the opposite side of the conveyance. "And you're right. One does not need your level of expertise to know that your relationship with Mr Thorpe is far more complicated than one would imagine."

Mrs Chambers snorted. "The man struggles to accept a woman might want to make her own way in the world. And of course, he finds my constant chatter rather tedious."

Sarah had spent the last hour attempting to assess Mr Thorpe's character. A man as austere and inflexible must surely conceal some past pain.

"Although I detest beards, I find Mr Thorpe to be quite a handsome gentleman." Sarah made the comment purely to gauge Mrs Chambers' reaction.

"That silly beard does nothing to show the line of his sculptured jaw," the lady replied. "And it hides the dimple on his chin that makes him appear far less stern." She scrunched her nose. "Not that he would care for my opinion."

The carriage rumbled to halt outside Madame Fontaine's shop.

"Mrs Dempsey invited you to take supper with us tomorrow evening," Sarah said as the lady climbed down to the pavement. "You must come while the gentlemen are out searching the streets in a bid to apprehend the villain."

Mrs Chambers inclined her head. "I would like that. It will occupy the time whilst we wait for news."

"Mrs Dempsey's coachman will call for you at nine." Sarah turned to Anthony. "Am I right in thinking you are meeting Mr Thorpe at nine o'clock?"

"Indeed."

Carter hovered on the pavement while he waited patiently to raise the steps and close the door.

Mrs Chambers nodded. "I shall wait at Madame Fontaine's. Please convey my regards to Mrs Dempsey. I do hope she feels better. She looked so pale earlier."

A sudden bout of nausea had brought about a headache and an urgent need to rest. "She was a little lightheaded. That is all."

"Then let us hope tomorrow will be a better day, for all of us. Good day, my lord. Good day, Miss Roxbury."

As soon as Carter closed the door and they were left alone, the air in the confined space sparked to life with an electrifying intensity.

The carriage had turned out of New Bond Street before Anthony spoke. "So, you find Mr Thorpe handsome. Should I worry? Should I be jealous?"

"I think most ladies find something alluring about myste-rious men. It was what attracted me to you."

His blue eyes sparkled with amusement. "Now you know my secrets, does that mean you find me less appealing?"

"Not at all." It astounded her just how much she wanted him. Even now, she could think of nothing other than his pleasurable touch. "Now I am intrigued to find a rather reckless gentleman beneath the prim facade."

"Prim?" he scoffed. A mischievous grin played on his lips. "What can I say? I was under the impression you admired my stiff exterior."

Sarah sucked in a breath. Never had she imagined they would converse so intimately. "I do. When the occasion deems it appropriate."

Anthony chuckled. "My body has a will of its own when in your company, Miss Roxbury. Indeed, you have lured me to sin. It is only you who solicits such a passionate response. You hold me captive. I am forever yours to command."

She liked the thought of exerting control, of having Anthony Dempsey completely at her mercy.

"You should not put ideas into a lady's head," she said. "The thought of having you pander to my wishes and desires is extremely appealing."

"That was my intention." He raised a brow. The silent communication told her he was more than willing to indulge her.

The moment of their first meeting flashed into her mind. The attraction was instantaneous. As soon as their eyes met, she knew they were destined to be together. "I often think of what would have happened had you not come to Hagley Manor that weekend."

"You do?" Anthony snorted. "In my absence, would you have formed an attachment to the captivating Lord Mannerly?"

"Of course not. While he is handsome, something is most

definitely lacking." No other man would ever make her feel as wonderful as Anthony did. "I'm afraid all men fall hopelessly short when compared to you. Indeed, I'm confident I will never love anyone the way I love you."

Anthony inhaled deeply.

His heated gaze devoured her.

Without warning, he crossed the carriage to sit at her side. "I would have a care. You know what happens when we broach the subject of intimacy." With his bare hand, he caressed her cheek.

"Well, you did promise to indulge my desires. If we are about to lose our heads, perhaps we should prolong the journey home." Her heart pounded so wildly it pulsed in her throat. "I think a long ride around the perimeter of the park should suffice."

"Love, you certainly know how to tempt a man." A wicked grin lit up his face. "So, you want to experience what it is like to ride alone with me in a carriage."

"More than anything." She placed her hand on his muscular thigh. Love had given her the courage to be reckless, too.

"You might find it a little bumpy."

She moistened her lips. "Then I shall just have to hold on."

Without a care for propriety, Anthony claimed her mouth. The kiss was wild, passionate. She could not taste him deeply enough to satisfy her craving.

"Good Lord," he said, catching his breath. "It seems that scandalous behaviour truly is in the blood."

Sarah leant forward and pulled down her blind. "Then heaven help our children." When Anthony cupped her cheeks to kiss her again, she chuckled. "Haven't you forgotten something?"

He glanced at his breeches. "I think we will have to work around the inconvenience of clothing."

Sarah sighed. "I was referring to Carter. You need to tell him we intend to prolong our journey. The last thing we want is a footman rushing to open the door and catching us unawares."

"Forgive my sudden lapse in memory. I'm afraid I lack experience when it comes to seducing a lady in a carriage." He opened the window and conveyed his instruction to Carter before closing it and pulling down the blind. "We have an hour," he said breathlessly as he dropped into the seat. "That should suffice."

Sarah slipped out of her jacket, untied her bonnet and placed both items on the seat opposite. "You appear to have forgotten something else," she said, gathering her skirt to sit astride him.

His warm hands settled on her waist. "I have?"

Sarah leant forward and kissed him with every ounce of love and passion in her body. "Indeed," she whispered as she broke for breath. "I think you'll find I am the one doing the seducing."

CHAPTER 21

*T*he main entrance to St. Margaret's burial ground was on Chapel Street, an area surrounded by almshouses built to provide shelter for the poor and elderly of the parish. Burial grounds proved to be the blackmailer's preferred choice of location. Perhaps the blackguard found it amusing to hide in the shadows and watch Anthony scour the weatherworn tombstones with his lantern, looking for an occupant named Emily.

Carter stopped the carriage on Stretton Ground as instructed. Anthony leant forward and wiped the mist from the window. The sky was but a vast inky canvas, the gusty breeze having blown away the rain clouds. The wet weather hindered him the last time, the slippery cobblestones making it impossible to run in boots.

In the dark confines of his conveyance, Anthony pulled his watch from his pocket and squinted to check the time.

Eleven o'clock.

After the briefing with Thorpe, Bostock and Lucas, they had gone their separate ways. Still, knowing he was not completely alone filled him with optimism. Indeed, this could be the last time he would succumb to the humiliation of being held to ransom.

His palms pulsed at the thought of choking the man responsible for months of misery. Yet, even in one's darkest hour, there was always something to be thankful for. His thoughts drifted to Sarah—God he doubted a lifetime would be enough to satisfy the all-consuming need he had for her. He closed his eyes and said a silent prayer to Fate for choosing to pluck his dream from obscurity.

A light rap on the window broke his reverie.

Carter opened the door. "It's time, my lord."

While his coachman always remained mute when it came to matters of his master's private business, Bostock had convinced Anthony of the need for more able men on the ground.

Anthony jumped down to the pavement. "You do not have to do this, Carter." He would not force his staff to do anything over and above their duty. "Your loyal service is all I ask."

"And my loyal service is all I have to give, my lord." Carter doffed his hat. "I'm happy to serve you in any way I can, though I don't know what use I can be."

Anthony patted his man on the arm. "All you need to do is keep watch at the crossroads of Broad Way and Orchard. I have no idea who will come to collect the satchel. You'll just have to use your instincts." He glanced at his man's wide shoulders and lean physique. "Remember, your job is to apprehend not maim."

"Aye, my lord."

"Whatever happens, if I do not return within the hour, take the carriage home and wait for me there."

Grabbing the leather satchel from the seat, Anthony swung it over his shoulder. It was heavier than he'd antici-pated. The notes were distributed between various books, slipped in between the crisp pages, which Anthony suspected was to deter the runner from understanding the real value of the bag's contents.

Carter disappeared to the front of the carriage and returned with a lit lantern. "Well, Mr Bostock reckons you'll catch the bugger tonight. And he seems like a man who knows his way around."

Bostock was certainly a man of some experience, and not just with his fists.

"Let us hope so," Anthony said, taking hold of the lamp.

He parted ways with his coachman at the end of Broad Way and walked the few hundred yards to the entrance of the burial ground. There were still people milling about, returning to their dingy rooms after long hours working. Those who'd spent the night supping on ale and gin staggered home. One need only venture into an alley to find a man asleep on the cobbles, or a woman eager to earn a few pence.

No one looked at him as he entered the gate. Nor did they question why a gentleman of his standing would want to creep around a graveyard in the dark.

The hulking black shadow of the church loomed over the tombs like an overbearing parent. Anthony scanned the morbid surroundings, wondering where to begin his search. There were close to fifty graves. The odd-shaped stones were sunken into the grass, randomly spaced. Some were short and wide, others tall and thin. Some were clean, pristine, others dirty and covered in lichen. It occurred to him that the stones were like human shadows, standing replicas of the grave's occupants.

With his lantern aloft, he scoured the epitaphs.

Damn it all.

Could people not think of different names for their daughters besides Mary or Elizabeth? Despite inspecting twenty inscriptions he had still not come across an Emily.

After ten minutes of desperate searching, Anthony found the grave to the right of the church, near a tree. In this tomb, the Emily remembered was a beloved wife and mother. A lump formed in his throat when he thought of all Emily Compton had lost at the hands of a lustful liar. Poor William would never know his parents. Harold Compton would turn in his grave, despairing at the situation.

Guilt flared.

Was there something more Anthony could have done to prevent the tragedy? Should he have acted sooner regardless of the consequences?

Anthony mentally shook his head. He could not think of that now. Sentiment weakened one's logic. And he needed his wits if he had any hope of putting an end to this nightmare.

Placing the satchel over the small carved stone, he turned and walked back out onto Chapel Street as instructed.

Lucas and Bostock were waiting at the west end of the street where the road merged into St. James'. Four alleyways linked Chapel Street to York Street. Predicting their quarry would head north, Thorpe had chosen to wait there.

Anthony headed east.

No sooner had he passed the perimeter of the burial ground than he heard multiple footsteps running behind him. He swung around to see three boys dart out of the gate. Holding his lamp aloft he noted one of them clutched the satchel.

Throwing his lantern to the ground, he gave chase.

While one boy continued towards St James' Street, the other two disappeared up an alley on the opposite side of the road. Despite his usual reservations, Anthony followed them through the narrow slate-grey tunnels. He dodged the open sewer running down through the middle of the cobblestones, almost slipped—on God only knows what—as he navigated the warren of back streets.

In the dark, it was difficult to see which boy held the bag. But Anthony knew the routine now. He knew they ran to meet the waiting hackney cab. Indeed, when the boys reached an open yard with four possible routes, they separated.

Taking a second or two to get his bearings, Anthony followed the boy heading north. Logic told him the alley had to lead to York Street. It was a prime place for a cab to wait.

With all the strength he could muster, Anthony raced after him, dodging barrels, batting away wet sheets left hanging on a washing line. A faint flicker of light up ahead suggested they were not far from the main road. Indeed, one minute he was within a few feet of his quarry, the next the boy was gone.

Charging out onto York Street, Anthony sucked in a breath of cleaner air, relieved to be rid of the putrid stench lingering in the alley. The boy pelted along the pavement in a bid to reach the waiting carriage.

The driver glanced back from atop his perch. With his collar raised and his hat pulled down low, it was impossible to identify him.

Hell and damnation!

The boy would not escape him. Not now. Not tonight. Not when this was his chance to put an end to his misery.

And then Fate chose to intervene.

Catching the tip of his shoe in a crack on the pavement, the boy tripped. With his arms flailing, he kept his balance though the incident gave Anthony an opportunity to close the gap.

Just as the boy reached the handle on the carriage door, Anthony caught him by the neck of his jacket. Overcome with a sudden surge of satisfaction, he pulled the boy clear of the vehicle.

"'Ere, put me down. I ain't done nothing."

"I'll have that satchel." Anthony grabbed the leather bag from the boy's grasp. "Now tell me where the hell you're taking these books."

The driver looked down over his shoulder. "There's no time now. Put the boy in the carriage." Thorpe's commanding voice caught him by surprise. "We'll speak to him away from here."

Where had Thorpe found the hackney? And what the bloody hell had he done with the driver?

"The lad was not working alone." Anthony tightened his grip on the scoundrel's coat. "Two boys got away."

Thorpe shook his head. "No one exited via the alleys, which means Bostock will have caught the one who fled down St. James'. With any luck, your coachman will have the other. Now climb inside before we attract too much attention."

No sooner had Anthony opened the carriage door and ushered the boy inside than the vehicle lurched forward.

The boy wiped his nose with the back of his hand. "I ain't done nothing wrong."

"What? Do you often lurk around burial grounds waiting for a gentleman to drop his bag?"

"You shouldn't have left it lying about."

"And you shouldn't have taken it."

Numerous times the boy tried to jump out of the moving conveyance. Anthony breathed a sigh when the carriage stopped, and Lucas and Bostock climbed inside with another boy in tow. Squashed onto a seat either side of Thorpe's hulking associate, both boys looked too terrified to breathe.

"There were three of them," Anthony informed. "One escaped through the back alleys."

Bostock did not appear perturbed by the news. "Then we must deal with things quickly." He draped his chunky arms around the boys' shoulders and gave them a bear-like hug purely as a means of intimidation.

Lucas leant closer, his cheek a fraction from Anthony's ear. "If we ever fall on hard times perhaps we could become enquiry agents."

"If we don't get to the bottom of this mess that might be the case."

The cab rattled to a stop alongside Anthony's carriage on Stretton Ground. It was apparent from the conversation that Carter had not thought to stop the boy tearing past him. Instead, he'd believed the culprit to be a drunken man cradling, what eventually proved to be, a loaf of bread wrapped in an old rag.

With a solemn face and hunched shoulders, Carter agreed to follow Thorpe's carriage to the yard of The Old Cock Inn.

Once at the inn, Thorpe climbed down from his seat and opened the door. "Wait in the yard for a moment," he said, addressing Anthony and Lucas. "I will speak to the boys alone."

"But surely—"

"It is not in your best interest to hear what I have to say." Thorpe's sharp tone cut through the cold night air. The white mist breezing from his mouth and nostrils made him appear far more intimidating. "The less you know about these boys and where they're from, the better."

There was little point being stubborn. "Very well." The only thing that mattered was finding the name of the rogue who'd been fleecing him for the last four months.

As soon as Anthony and Lucas vaulted to the ground, Thorpe climbed into the carriage and slammed the door.

Anthony glanced around the yard. Other than the odd coach and a few men gathered around a brazier most people were in their beds.

Lucas nudged his arm. "I'm surprised how quiet it is in there. While I don't take Thorpe and Bostock to be men who beat boys, I expected to hear raised voices."

"I assume one look from Thorpe will be enough to get the job done."

They stood in silence, staring at the conveyance. When it rocked on its axis, they stepped back just as the door swung open. Thorpe jumped down, followed by both boys. He reached beneath the voluminous folds of his greatcoat and retrieved a handful of gold coins.

"Here, a sovereign a piece and two for your master. What you do with your earnings is of no consequence to me. When I speak to your master again, I shall not mention your windfall."

Both boys stared at Thorpe in awe.

"Now leave before I change my mind."

The boys scampered from the yard, holding their caps on their heads as they skidded across the damp stones.

"Why the hell did you let them go?" Lucas complained.

A man of Thorpe's intelligence would not be lenient unless he had a damn good reason. "I assume they squealed."

"Like pigs." Beneath his beard, Thorpe's mouth thinned. Anthony realised it was the closest the man ever came to a smile. "They told me what I needed to know. They were hired to collect the satchel though they have no idea who hired them."

The unwavering sense of disappointment was like a

hollow cavern opening in Anthony's chest. "What? Please tell me you paid them to tell you more than that."

Thorpe raised an arrogant brow. "They were to deliver the satchel to Lord Barton."

In a sudden burst of rage, Lucas swung round and punched the air. "Bloody hell! I'll throttle the man when I get hold of him. I'll shove a bag full of blasted feathers down his throat and watch him choke."

Anthony narrowed his gaze. "Barton? You're sure it's him?" The feeling of immense satisfaction at putting a name to the culprit did not materialise. "I know I have limited experience when it comes to the criminal mind but I cannot imagine him killing Emily."

"Nothing surprises me." Thorpe raised an arrogant brow. "But I must agree. Instinct plays a huge part in my work. I feel the truth deep in my gut, yet something is wrong." He shook his head and gave a frustrated sigh. "Either way, once I've exchanged carriages and freed the hackney driver, we must speak to Lord Barton."

Twenty minutes later, they arrived at Lord Barton's townhouse in Portman Square. After an argument with the earl's butler, who made them wait on the doorstep whilst he roused his master, they were finally granted entrance.

"What's the meaning of this, Harwood?" Barton tied the cords on his velvet robe. "It had better be important."

"Damn right it's important." Lucas shot forward, his teeth bared as though ready to tear into the pompous earl.

Thorpe placed his hand on Lucas' shoulder. "I shall deal with this."

Lucas exhaled deeply, but inclined his head and stepped back.

Barton snorted. "And who the hell are you?"

"Well, I can be your best friend," Thorpe said in a menacing tone, "or I can be your worst enemy. Inform me once you've made your choice so we may proceed."

An uncomfortable silence ensued. Barton's eyes flitted around in their sockets. When he brushed his fingers through his unkempt hair, Anthony noticed Barton's hand trembling.

"I shall take your silence as a desire to be co-operative." Thorpe inclined his head. "Thieves have stolen something from Lord Harwood, five hundred pounds to be precise."

"Five … five hundred pounds?" Barton stammered. He appeared genuinely shocked. "Look here, if you're suggesting I had anything to do with it, then I must refute the implication fiercely."

Thorpe held his hands up. "I'm afraid we intercepted the thieves who were on their way to deliver the goods here. Why would they lie?"

"Deliver goods here? But that's preposterous." Barton's cheeks ballooned. He huffed and puffed. "You're obviously mistaken. I am expecting a package, but it is payment of a gambling debt."

Anthony cleared his throat. "Then tell us the name of the gentleman who owes you money."

"Why?"

"There is every chance he stole it from me to pay you."

"But it is not my debt." Barton put his hand on his chest. "I am to hold it on behalf of a friend who is to collect it in the morning."

"And your friend's name?" Thorpe said.

"I don't see how—"

"Do not make me ask again." Thorpe's face took on a hard, stone-like appearance.

Barton blinked rapidly. "It … it belongs to Mr Fraser. He's sailing to India on the *Falcon* and is calling in all of his notes. He asked me to take receipt of the package as he is occupied at the docks."

Bostock leant forward and whispered into Mr Thorpe's ear.

Thorpe nodded. He turned to Anthony. "Do you wish to pursue the matter with the constable? Of course, it will mean offering specific details of the theft."

Despite Thorpe's cryptic tone, Anthony knew what the man was asking. To press the matter further would mean revealing what he knew of Emily's death.

"No." Anthony sighed. The whole point of paying the ransom was to prevent a scandal. "I will accept Lord Barton's word as a gentleman that he knew nothing of the theft. I am certain neither of us would want to be the topic of drawing room gossip."

"Quite right," Barton replied. "Quite right."

"Then we shall leave you to return to the comfort of your bed," Thorpe said. "It seems we have an urgent appointment at the docks."

CHAPTER 22

*T*he clock on the mantel chimed midnight.

Sarah stared at the elaborate brass hands. Four or five times she had walked over to check it didn't need winding. Each passing hour felt as long and as tiresome as a whole day. Part of her wished the clock *had* stopped for the faint ticking taunted her like the ominous clanging of a death knell.

"Surely they will have caught the culprit by now," Sarah said for the umpteenth time before taking another peek out of the drawing room window.

Mrs Chambers took a sip of her sherry. "I suspect Mr Thorpe has forgotten all about the need to inform us of their developments. I'm afraid he likes to torment me whenever the occasion arises. No doubt they are celebrating with a decanter of port. Oblivious to our plight."

"You do appear to rouse his ire." Sarah recalled the enquiry agent's irritation whenever Mrs Chambers spoke. "One cannot help feeling you have known Mr Thorpe for a long time."

Mrs Chambers stared off into the distance. After a

moment of silence she said, "Well, Mr Thorpe and my husband were childhood friends. Indeed, the strength of their bond proved to be the reason Mr Thorpe offered marriage when Edward died."

Sarah swallowed down a gasp. She glanced at Helena asleep on the chair, feeling a desperate urge to wake her as she would want to hear this latest bit of gossip.

"Mr Thorpe must care for you a great deal if he offered his support."

Mrs Chambers gave a weak chuckle though any amusement failed to reach her emerald-green eyes. "Daniel thought it his duty to take care of me. And of course, he thoroughly disapproves of my work and would seek any opportunity to keep me locked up at home."

Daniel?

The name suggested someone strong and approachable, someone with faith in their ability to succeed whatever the task.

"Of course, the man is often too stubborn for his own good." Mrs Chambers sighed. "He refuses to listen to my opinion even though it would prove useful to the case."

The sudden thought that Mr Thorpe might not be as adept as he appeared sent a frisson of fear shooting through Sarah's body.

Sarah dragged herself away from the window and sat down. "Yesterday, at Mr Thorpe's house, there was something you wanted to tell him about the suspects. Was it important?"

"I'm not sure." The lady shrugged. "I was interested to hear his answer to a question."

Sarah studied her. She had the distinct impression Mrs Chambers was not entirely forthcoming. "And what question was that?"

Mrs Chambers sighed. "One must ask—where is Emily Compton?"

Sarah jerked her head back in surprise. Due to the distressing topic, it was not something she'd allowed herself to consider. She swallowed deeply. "What … what do you mean?"

Mrs Chambers opened her mouth to speak but then paused. "Have you ever spent time in a room with a corpse?" she eventually said. "Even after a few days, it is far from pleasant. Therefore, we must assume the blackmailer cannot be in possession of Miss Compton's body."

An image of a pale, lifeless figure flashed into her mind. Was Emily lying cold and alone in an unmarked grave? Had her killer hidden her in an icehouse ready to stage another scene to incriminate Anthony?

Sarah rubbed her temple to ease the sudden pounding in her head. "Do you have an idea where she might be?"

"I'm not sure. But do you not find it odd that Lord Harwood is forced to scour the burial grounds looking for a tomb containing a woman named Emily?"

Sarah sat forward. Once again, she contemplated waking Helena. Her friend would be eager to hear Mrs Chambers' opinion. "Are you saying you think the blackmailer wants Lord Harwood to find her grave?"

Mrs Chambers finished her sherry and placed the glass on the side table. "Yes. It is possible the culprit wants to be caught. The criminal mind is a complex thing. Indeed, we might never understand his motivation."

Heavens!

Sarah glanced at the window. "Well, with any luck, we shall know the answer soon," she said, feigning optimism.

Mrs Chambers tapped her finger to her lips. "I must say I am surprised at Mr Thorpe. He is usually so shrewd and perceptive. I would have expected him to conduct a thorough search of St. Margaret's graveyard as soon as he learnt of the location."

"Perhaps he is confident they will catch the blackmailer tonight."

"I hope he is right for there are far too many unanswered questions. Indeed, why has Mr Thorpe not raised the point about the crystal glasses? Surely their condition and the absence of a bottle would have pricked his curiosity."

"Oh, I doubt Lord Harwood mentioned the glasses. In truth, he did not notice anything strange about them. It was Mrs Dempsey who thought there was something odd."

They both glanced at Helena who was sleeping soundly in the chair. Despite numerous efforts to escort her to her chamber, Helena insisted on waiting for her husband.

"Then Mrs Dempsey is extremely astute." Mrs Chambers' voice carried a hint of admiration. "You said you found one clean glass and one stained with a burgundy residue."

Sarah nodded. "It could be nothing. It could simply be that only one of them drank wine or port."

"With the absence of a bottle or decanter, we might assume Emily was drugged before her murder. Perhaps the culprit washed away any evidence and took the bottle with him."

"Good lord." Sarah put her hands to her cheeks and sighed. "It hurts my head when I attempt to unravel all the relevant pieces of information."

The sound of carriage wheels rattling along the cobblestones captured their attention. Sarah rushed to the window and tugged the drapes, relieved to see Carter slowing down outside.

"They're back."

Helena stirred. She blinked and stretched. "Oh, thank goodness. My back aches from being cramped in this chair."

"I am struggling to contain my excitement," Mrs Chambers said. "There is something rewarding about solving a mystery."

Sarah turned back to the window, but her smile fell when the carriage failed to stop. "Where is he going?"

"What is it?" Helena asked.

"Carter has continued to the mews. I fear he has returned alone."

Without further comment, Helena summoned the butler and requested an audience with the coachman.

After a tense few minutes waiting, their impatience drew them out into the hall.

Carter appeared from the door at the end of the corridor. "I've come with news, madam." He bowed his head whilst gripping his hat in his hand.

"Yes, yes," Helena said curtly. "Did everything go to plan?"

"Aye, it did. They caught the young blighters running off with the satchel. Mr Thorpe questioned the boys and discovered they were taking the bag to Lord Barton."

"Lord Barton?" Sarah gasped. While the earl thought himself something of a catch, he didn't strike her as a man capable of abusing an innocent woman. Nor did she think him a man desperate for money.

"Aye, ma'am," Carter said. "His lordship has gone to Lord Barton's house in Portman Square. I've been instructed to inform you of the news and then return to wait for him."

"Then we shall not delay you any longer," Helena said. "And thank you, Carter, for keeping us abreast of the developments."

Carter inclined his head and stomped off in the direction of the servants' quarters.

"Just a moment, Carter," Mrs Chambers called after him, and he trudged back to stand before them. "You said boys, which obviously implies you meant more than one."

Carter looked down at his boots. "Aye, there were three."

"And does Mr Thorpe have all three boys in his custody?" Mrs Chambers' tone carried a hint of doubt. When Carter sighed, she added, "Children are used for their speed and agility. They work in groups for a reason. It would not be surprising to hear one of them managed to get away."

Carter struggled to make eye contact. "It was too dark, ma'am. The boy was too quick and light on his feet."

Nothing escaped Mrs Chambers' notice. Sarah stared at her, admiration filling her chest.

"Thank you, Carter." Mrs Chambers offered a weak smile. A look of apprehension marred her face. "You may return to your duties."

With sombre expressions, they returned to the drawing room and sank into their seats.

A heavy silence hung in the air. Lost in thought, they all stared at various parts of the pattern on the Oriental rug.

It was a minute or so before Mrs Chambers spoke. "There was another matter I wished to mention to Mr Thorpe. It concerns the Earl of Barton."

"Yes." Sarah straightened and focused her attention.

"It is said that Barton is unable to …" Mrs Chambers waved her hand in the air "… to perform in the way a normal man would. It is said he paid his last mistress handsomely to keep his secret. Indeed, Barton is on the hunt for a bride before knowledge of his delicate problem finds its way into the salons."

Helena frowned. "But if it is such a secret, how did you hear of it?"

Tapping her finger on her nose, the lady smiled. "I have yet to meet a modiste who is not party to the most scandalous gossip. Clients speak in the strictest confidence, of course, and I only reveal information I deem important. I shall attempt to speak to Daniel upon his return, but I doubt he will listen."

"Daniel?" Helena asked with some surprise.

"Mr Thorpe," Sarah clarified.

"It's hard to imagine Mr Thorpe having a given name. It makes him appear less intimidating."

A faint smile touched Mrs Chambers' lips. "I remember a time when he was rather charming. But I daresay he has witnessed many unsavoury things over the years that have tainted his view of the world."

Sarah considered Mrs Chambers' ebony hair and porcelain skin. She had a youthful glow to her complexion. Her eyes sparkled with vitality. Despite being a widow, Sarah suspected the lady was not yet thirty. Perhaps Thorpe's stern countenance was a mask for his true feelings; perhaps it masked a broken heart.

"Why should Barton's problem be of any interest to us?" Sarah asked, keen to return to the matter at hand.

Mrs Chambers shrugged. "It does throw doubt on his ability to partake in a liaison or to have fathered Emily Compton's child. Of course, there may be no truth to the rumours, even so, why would an earl become embroiled in blackmail? His estates are thriving."

"Then perhaps someone is blackmailing Lord Barton," Helena said. "It stands to reason he would want to keep his condition a secret. What if he is simply being used as a pawn in this game?"

"You make an excellent point, Mrs Dempsey." Mrs Chambers tapped her finger on her lips. "When you named the gentlemen on Lord Harwood's list you said two men arrived late to Elton Park. It would imply they travelled together. Just remind me of their names."

Sarah recalled Anthony's revelation with clarity. "Lord Barton and Mr Robert Fraser arrived after the other guests."

Mrs Chambers closed her eyes for a moment. Sarah watched the lady's lips move rapidly. The almost silent mutterings suggested a mind eagerly engaged in logical deduction.

Without warning, the lady shot out of her seat. "I must borrow your carriage." She flapped her hands as though eager to depart. "Forgive me. I know it is rude of me to ask, but there is something I must do."

"You know who murdered Emily," Sarah said, unable to contain her excitement. "Or at least you know the name of the gentleman blackmailing Lord Harwood."

"My mind often runs away with itself. There is every chance I have made a miscalculation. But I must pay a visit to the docks before high tide." Her gaze flew to the mantel clock. "By my estimation, I have a little less than four hours."

"The docks?" Helena frowned. "Why would you need to go there?"

"I do not have time to explain now, but suffice to say, Mr Robert Fraser owns an East Indiaman. It is a merchant ship named the *Falcon* which operates under licence to the East India Company."

Helena's blank expression mirrored Sarah's confused thoughts.

"I'm assuming it's relevant," Sarah said.

"While Mr Fraser has been seen in town, my source informs me he has vacated his lodgings."

Helena raised a brow. "He could have a mistress."

"Or he could be living on his ship." Mrs Chambers paced the floor. "You said Emily's torn undergarments were silk. No doubt they were ripped to give the impression Lord Harwood had purchased them as a gift and had consequently destroyed them in a jealous rage. Mr Fraser's ship imports silk. Indeed, it is the only ship he owns after losing his subscription in a card game. Where better to dispose of a body than at sea?" She waved her hand in the air. "I know no more than that. Madame Fontaine thrives on gossip but often omits vital parts of the story."

"But what will you do once there?" Fear and excitement coursed through Sarah's veins. She was tired of sitting around waiting.

"I shall inspect the ship." Mrs Chambers' eyes widened. "Oh, and I'll need a few items. Rouge, if you have any, and a knife or something equally sharp. And ask Carter for a length of rope. Failing that, a belt will do." She glanced down at her plain dress. "I'll need an old dress, something low at the neckline. It doesn't matter if it's too small."

Sarah gasped. She put her hand to her throat as her heart hammered against her ribs. "You cannot go to the docks alone."

The lady smiled. "I am more than capable of taking care of myself. In this line of work one must be trained to fight with fists."

Sarah's mouth fell open. No wonder Mr Thorpe appeared irate. She couldn't imagine the elegant lady delivering an angry curse let alone throwing a punch.

"Then I shall come with you," Sarah blurted, feeling a sudden urge to offer her assistance. Lord, she longed to solve the mystery so she could begin her life with Anthony.

"I will come, too," Helena said. As soon as she stood, she

covered her mouth with her hand. "Forgive me. I feel as though I am on a ship in stormy seas."

"You are with child," Mrs Chambers said. One did not need to be an expert to recognise the signs. "You must stay and rest. And the docks are no place for a lady, certainly not at night."

Helena dropped down into the chair, disappointment marring her pale face. "I would argue but I know I shall be a hindrance."

Sarah rushed over to Helena's side and grasped her hands. "Without you, we would be sitting here as ignorant as Mr Thorpe. Mrs Chambers would not have been able to make her deductions without your insight regarding the scene at the cottage."

Helena gave a weak smile. "I suppose you're right. Well, at least I do not feel so completely useless." She sighed. "But you cannot go, Sarah. If anything should happen to you, Anthony will never forgive me. Not to mention what Prudence will say for me being so lapse in my duty. Perhaps we should wait until Lucas returns."

Mrs Chambers cleared her throat. "I fear we might be too late. If Mr Fraser is the gentleman responsible, and he learns his plans have gone awry, there is every chance he will flee. We will never know what happened to Emily Compton. Lord Harwood will spend his days fearing another letter from his blackmailer."

Sarah knew that to accompany Mrs Chambers was an act of sheer lunacy. But she could not let her go out at night alone. Equally, Mrs Chambers was right. Anthony would not rest until he had caught the man responsible. How could he ever fully commit to her, knowing that his nightmare was far from over? And what of poor little William? Did he not deserve closure? Did he not deserve to know the truth?

"It could be hours before Lord Harwood returns," Sarah said. "Nothing will happen to me. Jackson will be with us. We will snoop around and report back should we find anything of interest." She glanced back over her shoulder. "Isn't that right, Mrs Chambers?"

"Of course."

CHAPTER 23

While Mr Dempsey's carriage raced along the cobblestones, Sarah and Mrs Chambers pulled the pins from their hair and rubbed rouge on their cheeks and lips.

A rush of excitement banished all Sarah's feelings of doubt and apprehension. Mrs Chambers possessed the ability to instil confidence with a simple glance. When a lady asked for a sharp blade in such a matter-of-fact tone, no doubt she was comfortable wielding weapons.

Done with her ministrations, Mrs Chambers sat back in the seat. She opened her cloak and tugged at the bodice of the dress that was far too small.

Sarah could not help but notice the lady's breasts spilling out over the ridiculously low neckline. "Really, Mrs Chambers, you look positively scandalous."

"Please, call me Daphne." A faint blush crept up her neck, the rouge on her cheeks disguising any further evidence of her embarrassment. "I feel like an elderly relative when you call me Mrs Chambers." She glanced down, almost shocked at the sight of her own body. "Good heavens. I do not know how ladies dress so provocatively. I feel positively naked."

"I assume that is the idea." Sarah bit down on her bottom lip. It was too late to worry. No doubt the enquiry agent was used to acting without thought for her reputation. "Are you certain no one will notice us?"

Daphne Chambers nodded. "Have no fear. People see only what they want to see. With loose hair and painted lips no one will recognise us, especially roaming around the docks at this time of night. I expect there will be but one man keeping watch on the ship. With our disguise, we will distract him sufficiently to gain access to the *Falcon*."

"Are we to pretend to be doxies?" Panic flared. The idea of being mistaken for a prostitute caused an array of vivid images to race through Sarah's mind.

What if they were accosted by a group of men, groped by filthy hands?

What if she became separated from Mrs Chambers and lost her way?

She could only imagine the look on Prudence's face if she learnt of her shameful behaviour.

"The streets surrounding the docks are brimming with women searching for sailors willing to pay a couple of pence for a tup," Daphne said. "For the men who have been aboard ship for months on end, it's the first thing they seek once on dry land." She gave a dismissive wave. "We are offering a service. No one will give us a second glance."

Sarah scanned the plush interior of Mr Dempsey's carriage. "Will people not think it strange that we travel about in such luxury?"

Daphne shook her head. The look on her face suggested Sarah was rather naive. "Many peers pick up prostitutes. I have already instructed the coachman that we intend to partake in a little charade. When we stop, you're to follow my lead." A smile touched her lips. "But whatever you do, don't speak. If you must say something, then I suggest you curse and mumble. Violent gestures work well, too."

Overcome with nerves, Sarah moved the blind and peeked out of the window. The bright lights of Mayfair were far behind them. Now, the streets appeared more chaotic, less structured. Houses were squashed together. The evidence of domestic life spilled out onto the filthy pavements. People sat in doorways. Children who should have been in their beds hours ago darted about in the road throwing sticks to a dog.

The world was tinged with a morbid grey mist.

"We shall be there soon." Daphne's voice cut through the sombre air.

"I hope our effort brings the desired result. Lord Harwood will be furious when he discovers we've come to the docks at night."

Furious was perhaps too mild a word.

"I imagine Mr Thorpe will be equally irate. And he will take great pleasure in telling me so." She sighed. "But my instincts tell me this is the course we must take, and they have not failed me yet."

Sarah could not help but stare in awe at her companion. Where did she find the strength to cope with such dangerous work? Was she not lonely? Was she not scared that one day she might not make it home?

"I know you would not break a confidence," Sarah said, "but how do you find the information you need? I imagine it can't be easy."

Daphne smiled. "You would be surprised how many ladies confide in their modiste. Madame Fontaine knows which men keep mistresses, what they write in their love notes. I hire pickpockets, boys to keep watch when I cannot be in two places at once. I use my charm as and when necessary. An eloquent voice, coupled with the right clothes, can achieve a great deal. The unwritten rule that one favour deserves another also proves to be useful on occasion."

"It sounds extremely complicated to me. Are there not better ways to spend your time?" Sarah did not wish her words to sound patronising. "I mean work that might be safer yet equally fulfilling."

Daphne's gaze grew distant. She blinked a few times. "My husband died under suspicious circumstances, though no one else believed it to be the case. Not even Mr Thorpe. What started as a desire to see justice served developed into a profession of sorts. And so here we are."

"I'm sorry about your husband." Sarah's heart ached. She knew how devastated she would be if anything happened to Anthony. "I cannot imagine what it is like to lose the man you love."

Daphne cleared her throat. "Ours was not a love match, though I cared for him dearly. Respect and kindness formed the basis of our marriage. Though judging by the way you look at Lord Harwood, I do not expect you to understand."

Sarah did understand. Respect and kindness were all she'd ever hoped for in a marriage. But nothing could compare to the feeling of love burning in one's chest.

"You might fall in love," Sarah said. She wondered as to Mr Thorpe's true feelings. "It is never too late."

Daphne laughed. "What husband wants a wife who dresses like a whore as part of her work?" She waved her hand at her bulging bosom. "Indeed, what husband wants a wife who works?"

Sarah raised a coy brow. "Perhaps a gentleman with the same ambition."

"You speak of Mr Thorpe?"

"Indeed. A partnership would make perfect sense."

"Except that he despises me and would—"

The carriage came to an abrupt halt.

Daphne peered out of the window. "We're here." She pulled down the bodice of her gown and sucked in a deep breath. "Are you ready? We'll need to let ourselves out."

Sarah gulped. "Yes. I'm ready."

They stepped down from the carriage onto the pavement adjacent to the Customs House: a large imposing Palladian-style building.

"Same time tomorrow night?" Daphne called out in an odd dialect. She gripped the carriage door as she spoke to an invisible person inside. "My friend 'ere can join us again if you like."

"Close the damn door," Jackson shouted from his perch. "Move, woman. Else you'll find yourself trapped beneath the wheels."

Daphne slammed the door and shook her fist at the coach-man. He flicked the reins, and the carriage jerked away before turning down the street on their left. Thankfully, Mr Dempsey's conveyance was unmarked. Even so, she could not imagine anyone accusing him of being unfaithful to his wife.

Left alone on the street, Sarah straightened her clothing, kept her gaze to the ground.

"Take my arm and keep walking," Daphne instructed. "We are to head down to the dock. I'll need to pay the man on the wicket gate. Due to pilfering, the quays are closed at night, although there will still be some labourers working. Thankfully, the revenue officers only tend to patrol the ships coming in from abroad."

"I assume those ladened with goods are prime targets for men with a mind for plunder," Sarah replied. Both fear and excitement coursed through her veins as they approached the wooden gate.

After partaking in a little salacious banter, a fee of a shilling and the promise to return later to service his needs, they managed to get past the guard.

"Men are so predictable," Daphne whispered as they hurried on their way. "One glimpse of a coin and a soft thigh and their morals abandon them."

They rushed along the narrow roads, past offices, warehouses and the wood yard. Unlike most places at night, the docks were a hive of activity. Men moved crates with wheeled contraptions. Another man led a horse pulling goods on a waggon. Raised masculine voices filled the air. No one approached them or made a comment until they passed a row of brick sheds with barn-like roofs and windows with spiked metal grills.

"What have we here?" A portly man approached them and blocked their path. His stained shirt hung out of his trousers, and the sickly stench of rum was overpowering. "Nice night to earn a penny."

Daphne moved to walk past him. "We're not touting for business. We've been hired by a ship's captain."

"I'll not be long." He chuckled, displaying a mouth full of rotten teeth. "We can go behind that shed there."

"We're already late." Daphne's tone was firm. "Move out of our way."

The man wiped his mouth with the back of his hand as his greedy eyes feasted on Daphne's exposed cleavage. As they tried to push past him again, he grabbed Daphne's arm.

Daphne stared at his filthy hand and smiled. "Now is that any way to treat a lady?"

"A lady?" He chuckled. A spray of saliva hit Sarah's face

and she heaved. With a dandified bow, he said, "Would madam like a fumble behind the shed?"

"If you let go of my arm I'll let you glimpse the wares."

He dropped his chunky paw. "Now that's an offer and 'alf, me lady."

Daphne bent down and raised the hem of her skirt. With lightning speed she pulled the knife from the sheath in her boot. Before Sarah could blink, Daphne pressed the silver blade to the man's throat.

"Ere, there's no need for that," he choked out.

"I suggest you crawl back into your hole." Daphne took a step forward, and the rogue was forced to step back. "My friend here carries a pistol, so I suggest you run. You have to the count of three before I tell her to fire."

Sarah stepped forward to stand at Daphne's side. With her hand hidden beneath her cloak, she pointed her fingers as though aiming her concealed weapon. "I'll shoot."

The man held his hands up, but his frantic gaze moved beyond their shoulder.

"One." Daphne did not need to count to two. The man scampered off down an alley between the buildings. She replaced the knife in her boot and brushed her hands. "There, that should—"

A gloved hand appeared over Daphne's shoulder and covered her mouth. At the same time, someone grabbed Sarah's arm and swung her around.

Her heart hit her ribs with such force it took a moment to absorb the magnificent sight before her. "Anthony? I mean … what are you doing here?"

Anthony's hard gaze had the power to turn Medusa to a pile of dust. "I could ask you the same question."

Mr Thorpe pulled Daphne back against his chest. "I am

about to remove my hand, Mrs Chambers. Might I suggest you try not to scream and shout."

Thorpe dropped his hand.

Daphne swung around, her ragged breathing evidence of a raging temper. "Don't you ever manhandle me in such a manner again. What possessed you to creep up on me like that? You frightened me half to death."

Mr Thorpe's gaze dropped to the excessive swell of creamy flesh bursting out of Daphne's dress. He swallowed, dragged his hand down his face and shook his head. "I assume your choice of attire relates to your work."

Daphne made an odd puffing noise. "What do you think? Have you ever known me to dress so scandalously?"

The corner of Thorpe's mouth twitched. Once again his gaze fell to her heaving bosom. "No. And I doubt I shall be able to shake the spectacle from my mind."

Daphne straightened. "If that is another one of your veiled insults then I would rather you kept your opinion to yourself. Now, we have work to do. I'm sure your line of enquiry proved to be a complete waste of time."

Rather than inflame Anthony's ire, their companions' volatile tempers seemed to distract him. Indeed, when Sarah looked into his eyes the only emotion she saw was fear.

"I'm sorry, my lord, if I caused you any distress." Sarah pursed her lips as she waited nervously for his reply.

Anthony sighed. "When we saw Lucas' carriage, I almost expired. Do you have any idea how dangerous it is here? Had we not arrived when we did, God only knows what would have happened to you."

Sarah lifted her chin. "Mrs Chambers had everything in hand."

"Damn it, Daphne," Mr Thorpe whispered through gritted teeth, oblivious to the fact he had used her given name. "Is it not enough that I watched you almost die once? Will you not be satisfied until you see me committed to Bedlam?"

"I am working, Mr Thorpe," Daphne replied haughtily. "It is not my intention to provoke you. Now, if you have finished lecturing me I have business on the docks."

"Obviously, you're here to inspect Mr Fraser's ship," Thorpe stated. "But I will be damned before I allow you to do so alone."

"Then you are free to accompany us," Daphne said.

Anthony cleared his throat. "I'm afraid Miss Roxbury will be returning to the safety of the carriage."

"What?" Sarah frowned. "I have not gone to the trouble of dressing like this for nothing. No. I am coming with you."

Anthony squared his shoulders. "No honourable gentleman would permit such a thing. God damn, why will you not accept that I act out of interest for your welfare?"

"I fear the female mind cannot understand the concept," Thorpe mocked.

Daphne shook her head. "We are wasting time. The more we loiter, the more chance someone will question our motive for being here. To take Miss Roxbury back to the carriage does not serve our objective."

"Please, Anthony," Sarah implored. "Let me come with you. Let me help you. This could mean the end to your nightmare and the beginning of a new life."

His steely gaze softened. He grasped her hand and pressed his lips to her bare palm. "I cannot lose you, not when I have waited so long to hold you in my arms."

Mr Thorpe coughed discreetly as he turned and stared out at the moored ships bobbing in the water beyond the basin.

"I will always be yours." Sarah struggled to speak. A sudden well of emotion filled her chest. "Nothing that happens here tonight will change that." She forced a smile.

"Besides, Mrs Chambers is extremely skilled in the use of weapons."

Mr Thorpe muttered something incoherent.

"We must hurry," Daphne said. "This is not the time for sentiment."

Mr Thorpe swung around. "For once, our thoughts are aligned."

"Very well." Anthony sighed. "We stay together."

"Might I suggest you all wait behind that brick shed." Thorpe nodded to the building behind them. "Once I have established the precise location of the *Falcon*, I shall return, and we can decide how best to proceed."

"How remarkable." Daphne smiled. "Those were my thoughts exactly."

CHAPTER 24

Thorpe appeared from the shadows. With the collar of his coat raised and his hat pulled down over his brow, the man cut a menacing figure in the dark.

"The *Falcon* is the third ship along. Only one man guards the gangway. I noted some activity aboard and suspect it is simply a matter of them waiting for the afternoon tide before setting sail."

"I can distract the guard sufficiently for you to gain access to the ship," Mrs Chambers said with her usual air of confidence.

To say Anthony was amazed at the woman's courage was an understatement. Indeed, she had proved to be more than a match for Mr Thorpe when it came to applying logic to a situation.

"If I can get close enough without raising the alarm, I could disable him temporarily," Thorpe said, ignoring Mrs Chambers' offer of assistance. "He would be unconscious for thirty seconds or so. We would need to slip past him before he wakes."

Mrs Chambers huffed. "As soon as you approach he will be suspicious, whereas I have ample assets to distract him."

The lady was not trying to boast. Even so, Thorpe struggled to keep his hungry eyes from gazing at anything else.

"Of that I am aware," Thorpe snapped.

"Then let me lure him behind this shed. Once out of sight you may do with him what you will. I have a rope for you to tie his hands."

Anthony raised a brow in admiration. "You thought to bring a rope?"

"We're wearing rope like a belt." Sarah parted her cloak and unwound the coarse length wrapped around her waist. "Mrs Chambers likes to be prepared for every eventuality."

"Indeed." Thorpe sighed. "Mrs Chambers seems to have thought of everything."

Mrs Chambers placed her gloveless hand on Thorpe's arm. "You must see that my plan has a much greater chance of success."

Thorpe stared at her. "That is not the point. But I concede to your superior judgement. Bring the man here, and I shall do the rest."

Mrs Chambers smiled and nodded.

"Do take care," Sarah whispered.

They watched the lady stroll out into the night. The seductive sway of her hips was enough to cause a rush of desire in many a man's loins. She stopped at the entrance to the gangway, parted her cloak to reveal all she had to offer.

The guard appeared more than eager to sample her wares. Cupping her breast, he shaped and moulded it in his palm.

"Damn the woman," Thorpe cursed. "Does she expect me to stand here and watch some brute maul and fondle her? When I get my hands around his neck, I shall take great pleasure in putting him to sleep indefinitely."

Anthony had never known Thorpe to be so emotionally unbalanced. "Have no fear. Mrs Chambers has stepped away and is leading the man here."

Thorpe flexed his fingers and cracked his knuckles.

As Mrs Chambers approached, they all shuffled back into the shadows.

"You'll not be in any trouble. You can still see the gangway from behind this shed." The lady's voice carried a licentious lilt. "If you're quick, I'll only charge you a penny."

Like a dog trailing after its master, the guard followed her behind the brick shed. Once hidden from view, Thorpe swooped in for the kill.

Thorpe punched the guard on the nose, hitting him with such force the unsuspecting fellow crumpled in a heap. "Lay your filthy hands on her again, and you'll not live to see daybreak."

Once down on the ground, Thorpe wrestled with the flailing figure. Applying pressure to a point on the man's neck, the restless body suddenly became limp and lifeless.

"Tie his hands." Mrs Chambers took the length of rope from Sarah and handed it to Thorpe. She proceeded to unravel another piece from around her waist and set about tying the guard's feet. Ripping material from her petticoat, Thorpe used it as a gag.

With the job finished they both stood, brushed their hands and gave a satisfied sigh.

"There we are." Mrs Chambers smiled. "A job well done, even if I say so myself."

"We should hurry before someone notices the man has left his post," Anthony said. "But I suggest we walk with purpose, with our heads held high. People only need note the quality of our clothes to assume we are taking passage."

"I am obliged to agree." Thorpe inclined his head. "To

creep around at night only rouses suspicion. To be bold is often the best policy. Besides, the crew will assume the guard gave us permission to board."

Anthony turned and tugged the edges of Sarah's cloak together. He bent his head, his mouth a fraction from her ear. "I am the only man who can feast on your creamy white skin." Despite needing to concentrate on the task ahead, in Sarah's company desire always simmered beneath the surface. Feeling an overwhelming need to touch her, Anthony grasped her hand. "Stay by my side at all times."

"By your side is the only place I want to be."

Her seductive tone conveyed a wealth of promise. Indeed, as soon as he'd dealt with Fraser, a vigorous ride around town in his carriage would be at the forefront of his agenda.

They all walked up the gangway as though they had every right to be there, waited until a few men moved up to the quarterdeck before approaching a seaman on the main deck.

"We're here to see Mr Fraser," Anthony said calmly. "He's expecting us. Can you point us in the right direction?"

"We arranged a little soiree for our friend before he sails off to India," Thorpe added. He gestured to Mrs Chambers. "I think he will appreciate our efforts."

The seaman's eyes widened as he gazed upon the over-inflated spectacle bulging out above the neckline of Mrs Chambers' gown. "He's more than likely below, in his cabin," the fellow said, gesturing to the hatch on their right.

No one questioned why they were on board. No one stopped them as they descended the narrow flight of wooden stairs. Once below deck, they navigated the passages until they reached the cuddy: a basic dining area servicing the roundhouse cabins situated on either side.

The room was empty. A solitary candle burned in its metal holder on the crude oak table. The surface was scat-

tered with various items: maps, dice, a flagon and two
tankards. Through the repugnant odour of overcooked vegeta-
bles, salt and rum, an overpowering floral scent hung in
the air.

Sarah gripped his hand. "There doesn't seem to be anyone
down here."

Anthony was suddenly relieved Thorpe had advised
Lucas and Bostock to wait outside Lord Barton's residence. If
they were wrong about Fraser, perhaps the real culprit would
appear to collect his money. But then a leather-bound book on
the table captured Anthony's interest. Upon examining the
spine, he knew it to be one he had used to hide the money in
his satchel the month before.

Anthony bit back a curse. "It would appear that Fraser is
our man after all."

Thorpe glanced at the book. "Then we shall sit and wait
until he returns. By the look of it, Fraser is the only passenger
on board. No doubt he will command this whole area. I
cannot envisage any captain relinquishing his quarters."

"Perhaps we should check the cabins," Mrs Chambers
suggested, a hint of suspicion in her voice. "At this time of
night, he might well be asleep."

Thorpe shrugged. "Only a fool would go to bed aboard
ship and leave the candle lit."

Ignoring his comment, Mrs Chambers moved to the row
of cabins on their left. She hesitated but then opened the first
door. With her hand to her mouth, she peered inside before
moving on to the next one.

Anthony decided it was best to be thorough and so
dropped Sarah's hand and began his search with the row of
five doors on their right.

The cabins contained nought but a bed, washstand and
night table. One small window provided the only means for

the occupant to breathe fresh air. Like the first cabin, the second room was also empty.

As he wrapped his fingers around the handle on the third door, the hairs on his nape prickled to attention. Through the thin partition walls, he thought he heard a low hum.

He glanced back over his shoulder and waved at them until receiving their attention. "I think there may be something of interest in here."

His fingers throbbed at the prospect of throttling the man responsible for months of misery.

They gathered around him as he held his breath in anticipation of what lay beyond the small wooden door. Easing the door from the jamb, he hovered on the threshold.

The sweet floral scent invaded his nostrils before he noticed the figure on the bed. Still dressed, the woman lay curled on top of the blanket, although her face was turned to the wall. Anthony's heart skipped a beat, but he resisted the urge to gulp for breath. From the wavy brown locks splayed over the pillow, he knew he had found the body of Emily Compton.

But the dead don't breathe.

The dead don't mutter to themselves or stretch their limbs in their sleep.

With hesitant steps, he entered the cabin, scanned her hands and feet for any sign of her bindings.

"Emily." With trembling fingers, he touched her arm. The heat from her body warmed his palm. "Emily. Can you hear me?"

She turned to face him though did not open her eyes. Not a mark or blemish marred the porcelain skin above her brow. By rights, there should have been a raised pink scar from the wound that had oozed so much blood.

"Emily," he repeated. The wild beat of his heart pounded in his ears.

Her lids twitched. She opened her eyes, blinked twice slowly before shooting up.

"My lord," she gasped. Her frantic gaze flew to the door, and he was aware of his companions stepping back into the dining area. "I … I … thank goodness you're here." She reached for his arm and clutched it tight. "I knew you would come. I knew you'd find me."

Anthony gripped her hand, relief flooding his chest. "I thought you were dead."

Fear flashed in her tired eyes. "I … I almost was."

"Where has he kept you these last five months?"

"I … I don't remember."

"Who did this to you? Was it Mr Fraser?"

She put her hand to her temple. "I hurt my head. Everything is a blur."

"Can you get up?"

A high-pitched squeal behind him captured his attention. "Let me go! Get your damn hands off me!"

Sarah!

Hearing Thorpe's string of vitriolic curses, Anthony swung around and raced out to the dining area.

He froze.

The terrifying sight before him stole his voice, robbed him of all sane thought.

"I'm afraid Emily won't be going anywhere. She is coming with me." Fraser pulled Sarah back against his chest, his other hand trembling as he pressed a blade to her throat. "Make one wrong move and I'll end it all now."

Emily appeared at Anthony's side, her eyes wide. "Robert!" She slapped her hand over her mouth. "Don't do this. Let her go."

"There's no time," Fraser spat. "We're to leave in a matter of hours. There's a pistol in the cabin, bring it to me."

Fraser was taking Emily with him to Calcutta?

Emily sucked in a breath. "What do you intend to do?"

"We'll bind them and lock them in a cabin, put them in a boat a few miles from shore."

Thorpe cursed.

Fraser was quite clearly deranged.

"I'll fight you with—" Anthony stopped abruptly. Suspicion flared. It suddenly occurred to him that Emily was far too familiar with her captor.

He turned to face her. "What happened to the wound on your head?"

"The wound?"

"Tell me, Emily. Where have you been these last five months?" His words brimmed with vehemence. Saying her name left a bitter, acidic taste in his mouth.

"My memory is not what it was."

He imagined grabbing her by her upper arms and shaking the truth from her deceitful lips.

Betrayal cut deep.

Damn her.

The boulder-sized lump in his throat was like a monument to humiliation.

"You're lying," Anthony snapped.

"I think it is fair to say that Emily is a partner in this crime, not a victim," Mrs Chambers said.

The words hit Anthony like a sharp slap to the face. It took him a few seconds to absorb the comment.

Had Lucas been there he would have punched the air, the wall, anything to release the anger building inside. As the tension mounted, Anthony repressed the urge to tear through the room like a whirlwind, destroying everything in his path.

The truth was the only thing he desired.

"You left your son." It was the one fact that had convinced him she was dead. Having grown up without her mother, he was astounded she would willingly hurt her own child in the same way.

Emily's bottom lip quivered. "Is … is he well?"

"As well as can be expected after being found cold and hungry in a blood-stained room."

"My lord, I—"

Sarah's dry cough echoed through the room.

Anthony growled. He shook his head to focus his attention. Only one thing mattered to him now. "If you do not release her this instant, I will not be responsible for my actions."

"Release her, Robert," Emily begged, "before you do something you might regret."

Something he might regret?

Was it not enough that he had taken an innocent woman's virginity, fathered a child out of wedlock, staged a murder scene and used threats to extort money?

"Be quiet." Fraser blinked rapidly. "What choice do we have? One way or another we are leaving on this ship."

CHAPTER 25

*T*he cold, sharp blade pressing against her throat was not what scared Sarah the most. Death was a far more terrifying prospect when one had something precious to lose. The pain of metal cutting into her skin would be nothing compared to seeing the man she loved fade away as she slipped from this world.

"If you hurt her, I'll not rest until I see you swing from the gallows." The tortured look on Anthony's face would haunt her dreams for some time to come. "Drop the knife and let her go."

"You should have stayed away," Fraser cried.

Anthony sneered. "Did you expect me to continue paying five hundred pounds a month? Did you expect me to sit at home and do nothing?"

"Tonight was to be the last payment," Fraser said as though it justified his behaviour. "We are to sail to India. Start a new life."

"Oh, you'll be starting a new life. In a cell in Newgate."

Fraser tightened his grip around her waist. "One way or another," he snarled, "we'll be leaving on this ship."

"It's too late, Robert. Don't you see?" Emily clutched her hands to her chest. "You must let the lady go. You must accept that Fate has conspired against us."

"No!" Fraser cried. "We're so close. We cannot turn back now. You must see that. We can use the lady as leverage."

"Like hell you will." Anthony gritted his teeth. "Let her go, Fraser, and will we discuss this like gentlemen."

No doubt Anthony's fists would play the leading role in the negotiations.

Fraser pulled her closer to his chest. She could feel his body shaking. Either he lacked the courage to use his weapon or his unstable mind made him unpredictable. The only thing to do was remain calm. But Anthony had the look of a man intent on murder and so she had to find a way to reassure him.

"Wait, Anthony. Give Mr Fraser a moment to think." Sarah kept her voice low and even. "I am sure he will do what is right. I am sure this is not how he envisaged it would end." She glanced at Daphne whose confident demeanour banished her fears.

"I agree." Daphne straightened. "I don't think Mr Fraser wants to hurt her." She took one small step forward. "Despite what we all assumed, Mr Fraser, you are not a man capable of murder." She glanced at Emily. "Anyone can see you are a man deeply in love."

A whimper left Emily Compton's lips. "We never wanted to hurt anyone. But we needed money."

"Be quiet," Fraser shouted. "Do you want us to hang?"

"It is a little late to worry about that," Mr Thorpe argued.

"We must all be accountable for our actions, Mr Fraser," Daphne added. "You do not want the love you have for Emily tainted by yet another wicked deed."

"Is it wicked to want to protect and provide for those you love?" Contempt infused Fraser's tone.

Daphne sighed. "It is wicked to hurt innocent people in the process."

"It is over, Robert." Emily wiped tears from her cheeks. "We were foolish to think it would be any different. We must pay the price for the terrible things we've done." A sob caught in her throat.

"Don't ... don't cry." Fraser's voice sounded croaky, uncertain. "I promised you a better life, and I mean to honour my word."

"A better life at my expense," Anthony countered. "But what of the son you abandoned? Does he not deserve your love, too? Has he not the right to know his parents?"

A high-pitched wail pierced the air. Emily crumpled to the floor. She clutched her stomach, rocked back and forth as her heart-wrenching cries filled the room.

Sarah sensed Fraser's anxiety. "Go to her," she whispered. "She needs you now, more than ever."

The words had some effect. Indeed, Fraser lowered his hand, the dull thud on the wooden boards an indication he'd dropped the knife.

Fraser rushed over to Emily huddled on the floor. "Please don't cry. Please. All I ever wanted was to make you happy." He caressed her back, stroked her hair. "All I ever wanted was to give you a home, a place where we could be together."

They all stared as the lovers wept in each other's arms.

The atmosphere in the room felt oppressive. Any satisfaction gleaned upon catching those responsible for Anthony's misery vanished.

Sarah clutched her throat. She could still feel the edge of the blade despite noting the shiny object on the floor. Her eyes locked with Anthony's. He closed the gap between them, took her in his arms and hugged her tight.

"If I'd lost you," he whispered, touching his forehead to hers, "I don't know what I would do."

She pulled away, put her trembling hand to his cheek. "But you haven't lost me, so you have nothing to fear."

"I doubt I'll let you out of my sight again."

Sarah nodded to the couple on the floor. "What will you do about Emily and Mr Fraser?"

Anthony shrugged. "My head urges me to punish them severely for what they've done. My heart is so full of love it begs me to show compassion."

"Perhaps if you hear their story it might help you to decide." She slipped her hand into his. "Come. Let us sit and try to understand how this all started."

Anthony nodded.

Sarah glanced over his shoulder at their companions. Daphne had wrapped her arms across her chest as if suffering from the cold. Mr Thorpe stroked his beard, his expression dark, brooding, his penetrating gaze focused on Daphne rather than the couple on the floor.

"Besides," Sarah continued, "these exaggerated displays of affection are taking their toll on Mrs Chambers and Mr Thorpe."

"Then let us help them in the only way we know how," he said. "Let us occupy their minds, find answers to our questions."

With a firm grip of Sarah's hand, Anthony strode over to the table and pulled out a chair. She sat, and he took the seat next to her. Following his lead, Thorpe held a chair out for Daphne.

"We'll wait at the table until you are able to join us."

Anthony's blunt tone cut through the air. "Then we will hear your confession. In full. In detail."

Fraser glanced up. "Regardless of what you believe, it was never our intention to hurt you."

"Then sit." Anthony gestured to the table. "Explain why you staged a murder on my estate. Tell me why you threatened to ruin my good name. Why you saw fit to rob me of my sanity."

Fraser helped Emily to her feet and guided her into a chair. He stood behind her, placed his hands on her shoulders. "We needed money. I have creditors chasing my heels. I lost everything but this ship in a card game. It was never personal. St. John offered me a partnership in an exporting business in Calcutta, and so I saw it as a chance to start a new life."

"Why blackmail me over a period of months? You could have been in India now, and I would never have uncovered the truth."

"To ask for such a substantial sum as two thousand pounds might have led you to call my bluff. Besides, St. John insisted we wait until he was settled. I could hardly tell him the reason for our urgent need to leave."

"We were going to pay back what we took," Emily blurted.

"The money is not the issue," Anthony snapped. "If you would have come to me with your plans, I would have lent you more than enough to cover your expenses."

Emily looked up at Fraser, frustration marring her brow. "Did I not say we should trust him? Did I not say he would understand? He would have helped us."

Sarah was overcome with the sudden need to speak. "I do not think either of you comprehend what you have done to an innocent man. He has spent five months in a constant state of worry. He isolated himself from his family and friends, spent sleepless nights wondering what had happened to your body."

Emily bowed her head. "I am ashamed of what we have done. I would have been happy to live in poverty. To live as a family with our son. But … but—"

"She deserved more." Fraser kissed the top of Emily's head. "Have you ever been blinded by love? Could you envisage doing terrible things foolishly believing them to be right?"

Anthony looked at Sarah, his eyes brimming with adoration. "I know there is nothing as important as true love," he said. He turned to Fraser. "And yes, I would do anything to protect the woman who'd claimed my heart." Beneath the table, Anthony clutched Sarah's hand. "I would hang to keep her safe. But I would draw the line at implicating her in a crime. I would draw the line at wittingly making my son a bastard."

Fraser swung around to face the cabin door. He rubbed the back of his neck and cursed. "Then you are a better man than I," he muttered.

They were the truest words ever said. Pride filled Sarah's chest. Anthony Dempsey was the best of men.

Mr Thorpe cleared his throat. "The question remains what does his lordship intend to do about the matter?"

Fraser rushed to Emily's side. He stretched across the table and clutched Anthony's sleeve. "Do what you will with me, but let Emily return to Elton Park."

"The time for heroics is long past," Mr Thorpe said coldly. Clemency was not in his nature.

Sarah stared at Anthony's profile. The corners of his mouth curled down, his shoulders sagged.

"Tell me what you propose to do about the boy you've left in my care," Anthony said.

Emily covered her face with her hands and wept.

"It is not our intention to leave our son indefinitely," Fraser said. "But we could not take him with us. The journey is hazardous. Disease is rife. At such a tender age he would be susceptible to illness."

Anthony sat back and folded his arms across his chest. "Do you not think he would be at greater risk at the orphanage?"

"The orphanage!" Emily dropped her hands. "You have not kept him at Elton Park?" She appeared shocked, astounded.

Fraser straightened. "Emily assured me William would be safe in your care."

While Anthony's expression remained impassive, he gripped her hand tight. "You must think me weak. A fool. You must think I lack the strength of mind to be selfish."

Anthony could never be selfish. It was not in his nature.

"On the contrary," Fraser replied. "We think you the most honourable gentleman we know. It might seem a ridiculous thing to say under the circumstances, but we respect you, hold you in high regard."

Anthony snorted. "Your actions imply otherwise."

Fraser dragged his hand through his mop of golden hair. "Had we thought you a fool, we would not have had to resort to such lengths to convince you of Emily's death."

Sarah pictured the stone cottage, the walls splattered with blood. "How did you make the scene appear so realistic?"

Fraser bowed his head. "We filled a glass with animal blood—"

"Please," Emily interrupted. "I do not want to hear any more. My lord, you have heard our story. What we did was wrong. But at the time, we were blinded by the thought of living a better life. We do not deserve your compassion, but I beg you to show mercy to our son."

Daphne sighed. "It is an impossible situation. The decision will not be an easy one to make. I do not envy you the task, my lord."

"A crime cannot go unpunished." To Mr Thorpe, there appeared to be no dilemma. "What is to stop them continuing their spree to gain money fraudulently?"

Anthony turned to Sarah, his expression grave. The deep furrows between his brows reflected the weight of his burden. She suspected he did not have the heart to send two friends to the gallows. Regardless of all he had suffered.

Sarah touched his arm. "May I speak to you alone for a moment?"

"Of course."

They moved from the table out into the narrow passage.

"What do you want to do?" she asked, although she already knew the answer. "Will you take them to a constable? Are you to rouse the magistrate and demand an audience?"

Anthony rubbed the back of his neck. "I don't know. I want to throttle Fraser for what he's done. Hell, if Lucas were here the gentleman would be a dead weight at the bottom of the Thames."

"But I sense your hesitation." She could not make the decision for him. There was but one solution that would satisfy him, that would help him to sleep soundly in his bed at night.

Anthony gritted his teeth. "He put a knife to your throat."

"In desperation. It was not his intention to hurt me."

He dragged his hand down his face and sighed. "What I want to do and what I think I should do are vastly different."

"I mean this as no disrespect to your brother, as I admire him greatly, but any man can use his fists to solve a problem.

Many men cite vengeance as a means to ease their conscience. You are not those men. Compassion is not a weakness. You must do what you feel is right."

Without warning, Anthony pulled her into an embrace. He kissed her once on the mouth. "Will you support my decision?"

Sarah stood on the tips of her toes and returned his kiss. "I will support you no matter what you decide."

"And if I … if I choose to care for William and let Fraser and Emily continue on their voyage?"

She smiled, her love for him flooding her chest. "Then I trust your judgement."

"Are you happy to live at Elton Park knowing William will be there?"

"Live at Elton Park? Is that another one of your cryptic proposals?"

"Perhaps it is time for clarity." Anthony lowered his head. The deeply passionate kiss robbed her of breath. "Marry me, Sarah. Marry me as soon as I can procure a special licence."

Her heart thumped wildly in her chest. It took all her strength not to jump about in excitement. "Now you have asked me properly my answer is yes. But we can talk about the details later. Let us return to the dining room and put Emily out of her misery."

Anthony nodded. "I have a feeling Thorpe might have something to say about my decision. He will not be pleased."

"Then we will have to distract his thoughts." Sarah placed her hand in his. "We shall let Mrs Chambers deal with him."

CHAPTER 26

"What I fail to understand is how you knew to come to the docks." Thorpe leant against the door of his carriage and folded his arms across his chest. His mood was much improved after the harsh words shared earlier.

Mrs Chambers glanced at Sarah. "It was not one particular piece of evidence that led me here. Indeed, it was pure guesswork on my part, although I always considered Emily Compton to be a suspect. It was simply a case of finding proof."

Thorpe swallowed. "Well, while I find your disguise highly inappropriate, I feel praise for your foresight is due."

"Praise? Did I hear you correctly?" A coy smile touched Mrs Chambers' lips. "Were I not so tired I would almost think that a compliment."

"Make of it what you will."

"What will you do now?" Anthony asked, feeling an immense sense of satisfaction upon discovering the truth, even if he had let the culprits escape punishment.

Thorpe shrugged. "I may take another case." He glanced at Mrs Chambers. "Should one pique my interest."

"I shall need a day to recover from the distinct lack of sleep." Mrs Chambers put her hand to her mouth and yawned. "Madame Fontaine is hosting a party tomorrow evening, and I promised to attend."

Thorpe's gaze fell to the lady's bosom. "I trust you will wear something more suitable, something less scandalous."

Sarah touched Mrs Chambers on the arm. "Such a fine figure as yours should not be hidden away in a dowdy gown. Then again, I am certain you would dazzle in whatever you wore."

"Indeed," Thorpe replied with a look of mild irritation. "Well, I should go and rescue Bostock from his post. No doubt he has fallen asleep in your carriage. Would you care for a ride home, Mrs Chambers?"

"Thank you, Mr Thorpe. It will save me the trouble of hiring a hackney."

Thorpe cleared his throat. "Is that your usual mode of transport?"

"We cannot all afford the running costs of a carriage."

Anthony suspected the couple's verbal spars brought them an immense amount of entertainment. Equally, he knew their abrupt manner merely disguised their true feelings.

"Can you tell my brother we'll meet him at home?" Anthony had no intention of going there directly. A ride around the park was long overdue. Besides, Lucas would need time to calm his temper once he discovered Fraser and Emily were free to leave for Calcutta.

"Certainly, although I would not care to be in his company when he learns the news."

Thorpe's disapproval was evident in his tone. A man with

such a hardened heart struggled to show even a sliver of compassion.

"Well, I think it takes great strength of character not to act out of vengeance," Mrs Chambers said, although Anthony could not decide if it was a compliment or a dig at Mr Thorpe.

"As do I," Sarah added. "Bitterness only rots the heart."

Thorpe yanked the carriage door open with such force it almost flew off its hinges. "It is rather late to converse on the street corner."

Mrs Chambers inclined her head. She stepped forward and embraced Sarah. "Well, I should be going before Mr Thorpe's verbal daggers penetrate my armour. Let me know should you ever make an appointment with Madame Fontaine. But remember, never tell her your secrets unless you want the whole world to know your business."

"Perhaps I might ask her to make a dress for my wedding." Sarah glanced up at him, love swimming in her delicate blue eyes.

God, the thought of giving her his complete attention caused desire to flare.

Mrs Chambers nodded. "I am sure she would be happy to oblige."

"We are yet to make any arrangements," Sarah said, "but please say you will both come."

"Nothing would keep me away." Mrs Chambers looked back over her shoulder. Thorpe was waiting inside the carriage. "I cannot speak for Mr Thorpe, but I will do my utmost to persuade him."

If Anthony saw Mr Thorpe again, he would be surprised. It occurred to him to offer the gentleman his thanks, convey his gratitude. But Thorpe had no time for sentiment.

Mrs Chambers climbed into the dark confines of the

conveyance. She waved to them as Thorpe's carriage lurched forward and picked up pace.

With Sarah at his side, and his gold-topped walking cane back in his possession, Anthony's heart felt lighter than it had in months.

He raised the cane and waved to Jackson, who was parked further along the road near a group of labourers using a wooden contraption to hoist a crate. Awake and alert, Jackson flicked the reins and soon pulled up alongside them.

Anthony opened the carriage door and assisted Sarah inside before conveying his instructions to the coachman.

"So, Mr Dempsey is using your carriage," Sarah said, appearing confused. "You travelled to the docks in Mr Thorpe's carriage, and now we are returning home in Mr Dempsey's carriage."

Anthony settled into the seat opposite. "We are not returning home just yet."

A smile touched her lips. "Oh, are we to go riding in the park?"

"Now I have you alone I thought it a shame not to take advantage."

"Is it not a little rude to use your brother's carriage just to satisfy your needs?"

"I did not hear you complain when we used his drawing room." Anthony couldn't help but smile. Never in his life had he spoken so scandalously.

Sarah studied him for a moment. From the deep rise and fall of her chest, he knew her pulse raced.

She untied the ribbons on her cloak, arched her back to present her ample breasts. "Can you spare a penny, my lord?" Her seductive voice made his cock jump to attention. "Have you time for a quick tup in a carriage?"

"Damn. I'd give everything I own for one night with

you." Anthony wiped his mouth. "But there'll be nothing quick about it. I intend to savour every second."

As the carriage rocked back and forth on the uneven road, Sarah gathered her dress to her waist and crossed the space to sit astride him. Anthony wasted no time. The first delicious thrust banished every dreadful nightmare, every sleepless night spent worrying.

"Tell me you do not think me weak and foolish for letting Fraser go unpunished," he said as he moved to rain kisses along her jaw. It was the last time he would mention it. But he would hear her reassurance.

Sarah sank into his lap, taking him deep into her core. "I admire you all the more for having the strength to make such a difficult decision." She sat up, let out a pleasurable hum as she took him into her sweet body again. Her head fell back. "Lord, I love you with every fibre of my being."

Anthony wrapped his arm about her waist, anchored her to him. "I have loved you since the moment I first met you. The last month has been torture. But the thought that we will never be separated again gives me great pleasure."

Sarah rubbed against him a little more frantically. "I … I don't want to return to Hagley Manor," she panted. "I can't bear the thought of spending a few weeks alone until we can be married."

Anthony could feel his control slipping. Conversation would soon be beyond his capabilities. "You're not going back there. You're staying at Elton Park with me. Hell, your whole family can come and stay. I'll do whatever it takes, but you'll sleep in my bed tonight and every night hereafter."

"How utterly scandalous, my lord."

"You're marrying a Dempsey. Scandal is in the blood."

Consumed by their passion, words failed them. Sarah

answered his plea with her body. The sweet smell of jasmine and orange blossom filled his head. The scent would always rouse feelings of warmth and comfort. It would always remind him of the battle he'd faced to claim his one true love —of the woman who had demanded his surrender.

EPILOGUE

ELTON PARK, ESSEX

The wedding took place in St. Bartholomew's: a quaint medieval church less than half a mile from Elton Park. While they had chosen to have a small select gathering, Mr Thorpe and Mrs Chambers had travelled from London at Sarah's behest.

Once the wedding breakfast was over, Anthony and Sarah mingled with their guests in the drawing room. In truth, he could not wait to be alone with his wife, but the novelty of having Mr Thorpe in their home proved to be entertaining.

"That boy is the image of the Marquess of Pulborough." Anthony's great-aunt Lavinia waved her walking stick in the direction of Mr Thorpe, whose awkward demeanour reflected his reluctance to interact with the guests.

At the ripe old age of eighty, Lavinia struggled to remember names. No doubt her eyesight was just as unreliable.

"Pulborough has hair the colour of honey," Anthony said. "Mr Thorpe has a more Mediterranean look about him."

"Not that foppish boy who inherited." Lavinia frowned. "His uncle. There is a painting of him at Pulborough Hall, sitting astride a mighty beast of a stallion. He was a handsome devil in his day. They have the same brooding look although Tobias was known to smile on occasion."

Anthony suppressed a chuckle. "I think you're mistaken, Aunt. While Mr Thorpe is educated and has impeccable manners, I doubt a drop of aristocratic blood flows through his veins."

Lavinia shook her head. "I'm telling you, put him in gold brocade and the likeness is uncanny. Now, where is your wife?"

"Sarah is conversing with Mrs Chambers." When Lavinia narrowed her gaze, Anthony gestured to the sofa.

"Lord, I could have sworn her name was Susanna," his aunt muttered as she ambled away.

Left alone, Anthony stared at Thorpe. His long, black hair was held back in a queue. The chiselled line of his jaw showed him to be a much younger man than expected. Perhaps time spent on the streets made him appear more experienced than his years.

A discreet cough disturbed Anthony's reverie.

"Have you nothing better to do than gape at Mr Thorpe?" Lucas said.

Anthony glanced at his brother. The satisfied smile Lucas had worn for days was still evident.

"I should go and speak to him," Anthony replied. "He is reluctant to partake in idle chatter with any of the guests. Other than the time he spends with Mrs Chambers he seems intent on standing alone."

"Perhaps the lack of a disguise makes him feel vulnerable," Lucas mused. "I contemplated tugging on his hair just to know if it's a wig. How on earth did you manage to drag him away from London?"

"I used emotional blackmail. I told him Mrs Chambers

insisted on coming, but I feared for her safety after hearing numerous reports of muggings en route. I suggested the lady would be likely to carry a knife in her boot."

Lucas raised both brows in a look of admiration. "You mean you lied."

"In a manner of speaking."

"Are they both staying the weekend?"

"No. Thorpe agreed to stay for one night. Mrs Chambers told Sarah they are working together on a case and could not spare the time. Indeed, I believe they have seen much more of each other these last few weeks."

"Well, Thorpe would be a fool not to make use of Mrs Chambers' deductive skills."

"Or seductive skills," Anthony said. "Sarah believes he harbours a deep affection for his partner. And I am inclined to agree."

Lucas glanced briefly over his shoulder and stepped closer. "You know Lavinia asked me if the rumours were true."

"What rumours?"

"That you've been brawling in public without your shirt." Lucas laughed. "I told her that while she should expect scandalous behaviour from me, she should know you would never degrade yourself in such a manner."

Anthony laughed, too. "I rather enjoyed being the rogue for once. And scandalous behaviour does have its advantages." When Lucas raised a curious brow, Anthony added, "When there are no spaces in the dining room at White's, gentlemen are quick to give me their table."

"White's," Lucas scoffed. "Am I supposed to be impressed?"

Anthony shrugged. "If rumours are to be believed I hear you have some news."

"News?" Lucas frowned. "I am at a loss, although I'm sure you're about to enlighten me."

"It appears some people know you as Captain Lawrence. When did you spend time in the military?"

Lucas chuckled.

"Sarah's grandfather is delighted to know she will be related to such a prestigious captain," Anthony continued. "He doesn't give a damn she married a viscount."

Max Roxbury had explained the reason for the confusion, that it had come about during the party at Roxbury Hall, but Anthony enjoyed teasing his brother.

"You really must get out more," Lucas said. "Do you not know it is an acting game played in all the best houses?"

"I cannot imagine playing it here." Anthony glanced at the lonely figure of Mr Thorpe. "I could not see Thorpe doing anything that might raise a smile. I should go and rescue him before Lavinia pounces and bombards him with probing questions about the Marquess of Pulborough."

"Pulborough?"

"Never mind."

Lucas clutched Anthony's sleeve. "It's your wedding day. I'll act as Thorpe's chaperone. I can see you are itching to give your wife her wedding gift. I hope it will make up for the fact she's shackled to you."

"I'm certain she'll be pleased." Anthony patted his brother on the arm. "And no doubt Thorpe will be delighted to hear all about your military career."

Lucas cocked a brow. "With my training in subterfuge, I shall cover for you for half an hour." He gave a wicked grin. "Or for an hour if you're so inclined."

For the hundredth time in the space of a few hours, Anthony's gaze drifted to Sarah.

God, she was so damn beautiful.

As though drawn by the power of thought alone, she looked up and met his gaze. He jerked his head, gestured to the door. She smiled in the coy way that made him struggle to catch his breath.

He stared in awe as she walked over to him. "I hate to tear you away from our guests, but do you think you could spare your husband a few moments of your time?" He slipped his hand into hers. "There is something I want to show you."

A seductive smile played on her lips. "How can I refuse such a tantalising offer?"

They made their way through the house and out into a secluded corner of the garden.

"Please tell me you have not been snooping down here?" Anthony said. Excitement bubbled in his chest as he anticipated her reaction to his surprise.

Sarah shook her head. "Helena urged me not to."

They came to a stop outside the summerhouse. Lucas had spent the last two weeks helping him redesign the small space. Indeed, Anthony had paid the carpenter and glazier from Witham double their usual fee to make sure it was finished on time.

"Close your eyes," he said, but then covered them with his hand as he expected her to peek.

Sarah giggled.

Anthony opened the door of the small wooden building and guided her around the edge of the room.

"Can I open my eyes?" Excitement was evident in her voice.

Anthony dropped his hand. "You may open them now."

For a moment she simply stared. Then her wide-eyed gaze moved up to the glass ceiling, to the telescope positioned in the corner, to the sunken bed of cushions in the middle of the floor.

Nerves practically choked him. "Do you like it? I thought we could come here after dark, lie down and observe the blanket of stars. I'm assured this is a prime position to observe many constellations."

She turned to him. A tear trickled down her cheek.

"Is something wrong?" he asked as panic flared.

"No." She put her hand over her heart. "It is the most wonderful thing I have ever seen."

Anthony wiped away her tear. "Then why are you crying?"

She sucked in a breath as she put her hand on his cheek. "Because I am so in love with you I feel my heart is ready to burst out of my chest."

He swallowed down the lump in his throat. "You are everything to me. I shall spend my life making up for those times when I appeared indifferent, when I kept my love for you a secret." He lowered his head and kissed her slowly, deeply, with a wealth of passion. "I love you. You will never have cause to doubt me again."

She looked down at the mound of cushions. "Is it comfortable?"

"Would you care to lie down and make an assessment?"

As soon as the playful smile touched her lips, he knew her answer. "Do we have time?"

"We have a lifetime."

"Then you should lock the door. It would not do for a footman to enter and catch us unawares."

Anthony rushed to the door, turned the key and pulled down the blind. He turned to face her, desperate to feel the warmth of her naked body. "Then let us hope Captain Lawrence can distract the guests sufficiently."

"Captain Lawrence?"

"He's a relative of mine. It seems military tactics are in the blood. We both know what it means to surrender."

THE END

Books by Adele Clee

To Save a Sinner

A Curse of the Heart

What Every Lord Wants

The Secret To Your Surrender

A Simple Case of Seduction

Anything for Love Series

What You Desire

What You Propose

What You Deserve

What You Promised

The Brotherhood Series

Lost to the Night

Slave to the Night

Abandoned to the Night

Lured to the Night

Lost Ladies of London

The Mysterious Miss Flint

The Deceptive Lady Darby

The Scandalous Lady Sandford

The Daring Miss Darcy

Avenging Lords

At Last the Rogue Returns

36342698R00152